THE END OF THE CIRCUS

A Tale of Awakening

Michael Kares

Copyright © 2020 Michael Kares

The characters and events portrayed in this book are fictitious. Any similarity to real persons, living or dead, is coincidental and not intended by the author.

No part of this book may be reproduced, or stored in a retrieval system, or transmitted in any form or by any means, electronic, mechanical, photocopying, recording, or otherwise, without express written permission of the publisher.

ISBN-13: 979-8610015613

*To the seen and unseen, whose love has inspired
me to express my soul on these pages.*

PROLOGUE

Five-year-old Jabari awoke to the smell of sweet porridge, and the sound of excited voices growing louder as they approached his village home. He crawled out of bed and sidled next to his tall, powerful father who opened the door. Jabari saw children from his village surrounding several light-skinned, uniformed men with long guns. A dark-eyed, mustached man stepped forward. "Are you the tracker!" Jabari clung to his father's leg.

His father eyed the man cautiously and put a hand on Jabari's head. "Yes … I'm Akala."

The man's mustache twitched. "We're looking for lions—we need your help."

Akala's eyebrows drew together as he glanced toward Jabari's mother. "Let's talk," and led them away from the house. He returned a brief time later and announced to the family: "I'm going on an expedition tomorrow."

Jabari's mother turned from her food preparations, clenching her dishcloth. "Are you sure about this, Akala?"

"It will only be a few days," he said persuasively.

She turned back to her cooking pot and stirred stiffly. "I don't like this," she quipped.

Akala crossed his arms over his chest. "You know we need the money."

She shook her head and looked back at her husband with imploring eyes. "Akala, I have a bad feeling about this."

"Don't worry…everything will be fine."

His reassuring, yet closing tone put an end to the discussion, allowing Jabari to ask his father a question: "Why do they want to kill the lions, Father?"

"They don't want to kill them, Jabari…" His father roared like a lion. "… They want to capture them!" He wrapped his boy in his arms, launching Jabari into laughter. Akala placed a hand on the back of his son's neck and playfully shook him from side to side. He then rubbed his head affectionately and left to prepare.

The following day, Akala arose before the sun, gave sleeping Jabari a gentle kiss on his forehead, said a soft, "I love you," and departed.

That day continued as normal for Jabari; school and play in the morning, lunch at home with his mother, followed by more school and play in the afternoon under the shade of an enormous baobab tree. On the second day, while poking at his evening meal, he paused with sadness in his deep brown eyes. "Will father be home tonight to read to me?"

"I hope so."

But his mother had a strange look on her face that Jabari hadn't seen before, and something about how she said it made his stomach even more uneasy.

On the afternoon of the third day, while playing under the grand tree, Jabari saw the same uniformed men leaving his home. He darted toward his house, crossing the path of the man he'd seen talking with his father days before. But he paused at the door—he could hear his mother crying—and when he pressed it open, his eyes confirmed it; She sat on the earthen floor, head down, sobbing. As Jabari edged closer, he saw her tear-streaked face overlooking scattered pieces of rectangular colored paper. She gathered Jabari in her arms and told him something that would take him a long time to comprehend; his father was never coming back.

❋ ❋ ❋

The time that followed was very difficult for Jabari and his mother. As the days turned into weeks, and the weeks into months, they did their best to cope, but they felt empty inside. Their daily lives had the same routine outline, but not the same content. Gone was the laughter and joy they'd shared, and in its place was a constant longing for what they'd once had. They did their best to manage by continuing with many of their favorite rituals, one of which was reading to Jabari before bed.

"Read another page, please read more!" pleaded young Jabari, his eyes eager and serious.

She closed the book gently. "It's time for bed now, Jabari. I'll read more to you tomorrow," she whispered.

Jabari grabbed the book from his mother and hugged it close. She cupped his tiny head with her hand and stroked his temple with her thumb.

He didn't understand what it was, but something moved him whenever she read from the pages of his most treasured possession—a gift from his father. He knew many of the animals in the story. Elephants, zebras, monkeys, and lions were part of his everyday life in the savannah. That wasn't what fascinated him. What called to him was the intrigue and mystery of the unknown; the allure of things he hadn't experienced. The book projected images onto the screen of his imagination of the grandeur of the circus: mysterious people from far-off lands; important guests from the cities entertained by the spectacle of the shows. He longed for something he couldn't explain; that somehow, by following its call, he would feel different. This desire ran much deeper than his mind could acknowledge. Deep below the surface of his thoughts and feelings about the circus lay an undefined hope. The gravity of which pulled on him, drawing him closer to that which he couldn't express: He wanted to feel anything, other than the deep flowing sadness of a boy without the love of his father.

As the waves of sleep flowed over him, he thought of those people in far-away places. People with fine clothes and big houses who, if only for a short while, wanted to escape their world into that of another.

An idea much larger than Jabari drifted through his sleepy mind; it puzzled him that those who had so much were also looking for something. *Perhaps everyone is trying to find something,* he thought to himself. As the book rose and fell against his torso, his mother whispered to him, the *Song of the Stars*:

> *Do not be afraid; you are never alone.*
> *We shine from above, to guide you home.*
> *When you are troubled, look up to the light,*
> *To find your way, through the darkest night.*

ONE

Jabari passed the quiet evening tending to the animals with no one to listen to or watch. He usually fed and watered them while observing the performers practice, or cleaned a wagon stall long enough to overhear a tale of adventure—tales too incredible to believe, were it not for the storyteller's swearing that they'd seen it with their own eyes.

The cast of characters of his camp life were absent this evening, and during the months he'd been a part of the traveling group, he enjoyed them; laughing jugglers as they practiced tossing their batons; strange accents of powerful and toned acrobats as they tumbled and contorted their bodies.

But the solitude of this night gave rise to emotions he'd rather avoid; feelings that a busy camp life would normally drown out. As his sadness overcame him, he could not ignore how lonely he felt.

At home, he'd yearned with teen angst to escape the monotony of his dull village, until his hope for adventure became a promise that only far-away lands and foreign people could fulfill. When he ran away those many months ago, he went as far as possible; his blood coursing with a passion for adventure, but with each friendless day, it dripped from him. What was once new, was no longer, and now, a longing to return to his own place and people flowed. Home, where he was accepted. Home, where he was loved. Home, where he felt safe. Home was where he wanted to be, now more than ever.

The money he had taken from his mother—blood money,

as she once called it, that she kept in a sacred box, but refused to spend—he consumed on one-way passage. Knowing that it would be a very long time before he could afford the lengthy journey home made his sadness even greater. Like the animals for which he cared, he too was trapped.

When the ringmaster announced the celebration for the fifteenth anniversary of The Malcolm Brothers Spectacular Traveling Circus, to be held at an extravagant hotel, Jabari resolved he wouldn't go. He had no fine clothes to wear, and no friends he could enjoy it with. *Who would tend to the animals*? he justified to himself. No, he'd stay; he knew his place. He was a stable hand, and he didn't belong at such a party.

Jabari's routine was to work his way from the first of the trailers in the caravan, to the last. First cleaning out the stall and then providing food and water. He did it with kind attention to the creature as well as the action, all the while singing a song from his childhood to his captive audience. He sang so softly that it was barely perceptible, but it was touching and pure. His voice held something special that was inexplicable—like all gifts, it was both him and something more—felt as much as heard.

Jabari imagined his singing soothed the animals—he knew it soothed him. Perhaps it was both. Something about the animals also comforted him, and despite his undesirable position, he enjoyed the opportunity to tend to them. It may have been a sense of purpose, being able to help those who couldn't help themselves. Or was it a kinship because the animals reminded him of himself—trapped and far from home? Or perhaps it was because he knew they wouldn't judge him for being different, as many in the circus had. Alas, it may have been all these things, but whatever the reason, he enjoyed being around them, and this kept him there longer than he had expected.

The circus trailers formed a wall behind the giant white tent, with a moat of trampled grass separating the two. The greenery was just wide enough to guide even the largest of animals in and out of the great tent's rear entrance for each performance.

When Jabari arrived at the first of the last four trailers, he saw the Malcolm brothers' shadows, cast as giants against the inside of the canvas, by a lantern, low and at the far side of them. The younger and more outgoing of the two was the ringmaster. With an aptitude for showmanship, and a flair for the dramatic, he loved what he did so much that he always wore his top hat; the shadow of which now stretched up to the tent ceiling. The older Malcolm brother was more reserved and handled the business of running the circus. This Malcolm always wore a fine waistcoat with striking adornments, which made his shadow against the white fabric look like a giant general with broad, exaggerated shoulders.

Jabari furrowed his brow at their sight. *Of all people, they should be at the celebration,* he thought to himself. He couldn't hear what they were saying but thought *it must be important,* to keep them from the grand party, marking their many years of success together. Rather than disturb them, and risk their ire, he ceased working and lay atop the bales of stacked hay between the trailers next to him. He didn't know when the performers would return, but assumed it would be late, being a once-in-a-lifetime event.

❋ ❋ ❋

Jabari awoke to the warm light of the sun upon his eyelids, his loneliness consoled by thoughts of a busy and distracting day. He heard the animals making their usual morning noises, then realized he wasn't in his bed—he was still upon the hay between the trailers. Dread gripped his heart. *I fell asleep and forgot to take care of the animals!* Fear burst into his groggy mind. *I'll be thrown out of the circus!* He opened his eyes and snapped upright. But something else was wrong. It was still dark, and the light wasn't the morning sun. It was fire.

The front of the tent nearest to the first trailer was ablaze and the bales of hay and straw that lay next to each animal trailer were roaring, swirling balls of flame; so were the straw piles closing the far opening between the trailers and the tent. Within seconds, flames danced in a line across the tent fabric, moving in his direction. He realized that the animal sounds he had heard earlier were the sounds of panic: horses kicking and whinnying, and dogs barking. The inferno roared through the grassy moat like a merciless dragon. The beast devoured the oxygen and spewed black, acrid smoke. Trapped in their trailer cages, with the bars open to the flames, the animals were helpless. Unable to breathe and with no way of escape, they fell silent.

    Jabari didn't remember hearing the performers return from their party, and he could no longer see Mr. Malcolm or the Ringmaster. "Fire!" he shouted. "Fire!" Silence save for the animals and the crackle of the flames. *No one is here to help*! He jumped off the hay bales, and his eyes glimpsed the stars beyond the glowing flames. He grabbed the keys that lay where he slept and began opening the trailers, starting with the one next to him. Frantically, he thrust its key into the lock and unsnapped it. Ripping the chain over the bars, he then pulled open the enormous steel door, until it continued to open under the momentum of its own weight. As he ran to the next trailer, a monstrous African elephant stepped out. She held her trunk low between her glowing white tusks to draw in clean air. Jabari didn't care that *Ellie,* as she was called, was loose. He only cared that she was able to escape the flames and suffocating smoke.

    He twisted the key to the second trailer lock when he saw that the fire now fully consumed the trailers earlier in the line. The tent itself continued to burn, snaking in lines across the fabric, threatening to dissuade him from his task as the hay bales nearest him ignited. He unlocked the gate and swung it open. *Z*, a panicked zebra, darted out, hitting the half-open gate, throwing Jabari to the ground. Z galloped away from the flames, past the last two trailers, to the open field beyond the burning tent. His white stripes glowed in the light of the flames as he paced in circles in shock.

THE END OF THE CIRCUS

The third trailer was similar, but smaller and with an older lock than the others, which made it faster for Jabari to find the matching aged key, but unlike the other locks, it was stiff and difficult to open. After struggling with it as he expected from experience, he unlatched the lock and swung open the creaking, rusty gate. Nothing moved at first, and then, in the darkest corner, away from the light of the flames, he saw his friend ambling toward the door.

Jabari coughed as he reached out his hand, "Quickly, O!" A long arm swung from below and stretched what appeared to be the depth of the trailer itself to Jabari. This was his most beloved creature, an aged orange and gray orangutan with warm, soft eyes and gentle confidence. He took Jabari's hand and stepped as fast as his frail body could take him. He teetered from side to side as he walked out of the wheeled cage, past the last trailer, and joined the zebra in the field.

Adrenaline was coursing through Jabari, but now fear seized him—the heat and smoke were suffocating as the bales behind him blazed with increased momentum. With the last key in his hand, he had to decide if he should stop now, satisfied with what he'd done, or risk his life and try to open the last trailer. Had it been any other animal, he would've continued without hesitation, but as it was, he paused before deciding. He couldn't leave an innocent animal to die a cruel and undeserved death, when it was in his power to help. But this final trailer housed no such creature—this was the animal Jabari feared the most—not unlike the one that had taken the life of his father. And this *Lefu*, had a reputation: Jabari had overheard tales of performers and stable hands who'd found themselves at the pointed end of this killing machine. Legend or not, he was as frightened to open the door as he was of the inferno upon him.

He closed his eyes; for the acrid smoke, or fear of the lion, he wasn't sure. He felt the lock, inserted the key and twisted it, then he released the latch, pulled open the door and fell to the ground, coughing. *If the lion doesn't devour me, the flames surely will,* thought Jabari, and he passed out in front of the open cage.

TWO

Jabari stirred, and what began as a clearing of his throat became a hacking, wheezing, spitting cough that burned his throat and he recoiled in pain with each strained breath. He took a moment to gather himself, unscrewed the cap from the canteen around his neck, and sipped with relief while he assessed his surroundings. Ash smeared his dark skin and dirt covered his black curly hair on one side, but apart from his lungs, he felt okay. He sat in a small clearing in a forest, blanketed in mist, near the elephant and the orangutan. The haze covered the elephant's legs and eclipsed the orangutan's body, showing only his striking, wide face. The moon cast a dim light, creating a soft ethereal glow upon the fog, making the orangutan appear as a floating-head apparition next to the majestic elephant. Jabari had no idea how he got there, and no idea where here was.

"You burn bad?" said the old orangutan to the elephant in his pidgin Malaysian dialect.

The elephant giggled. "…No, thank you, nothing a little mud won't heal," in a gentle, lilting voice.

Jabari coughed again and Ellie flushed. "I tried to get him out of there as fast as I could."

"You do good," said O.

Ellie tucked her trunk low and put her front legs together. "Thank you."

Jabari looked at Ellie and O with wide eyes. "Am… I dead?"

Ellie exhaled a quick laugh, then became quiet as if she'd overstepped her place—she'd been well trained not to do that.

O turned his head slowly and looked at the boy, "Your pain tell me no."

The absurdity of what he was experiencing dawned on Jabari. *Am I dreaming?* He paused to absorb what was happening. "So how is it that I can talk with you?"

"Maybe you no listen before," said the orangutan slowly and gently.

Jabari didn't have time to respond as at that moment, Lefu stepped into the clearing from the forest. "We are safe here for now. Z agreed to watch from the woods and will let us know if he sees anyone coming to look for us."

Terrified of the lion and unable to reconcile what he was experiencing, Jabari fainted again. When he awoke, he found himself on the ground and in the company of the elephant, the orangutan, and the lion. They hadn't noticed that he'd awakened, and he lay still, eyeing them.

"We can't stay here," said the lion, looking at O for a response.

O stood with a thin smile, relaxed.

Ellie swayed her trunk back and forth and avoided eye contact with Lefu.

Lefu looked at Ellie. "What do you think?"

"Don't ask me," Ellie blurted. "I don't know what to do."

Z marched from the forest and joined the group. "We need a plan!" Z spoke like a soldier and it came out as a command.

"*Really,*" said the lion sarcastically. "Of course, we need a plan; tell us something we don't know."

Jabari snickered, but caught himself, closed his eyes, and fell quiet again. He waited in the silence that followed, hopeful that they'd not heard him. Unable to wait any longer, he released the pressure from his eyelids to let in just enough light to see their silhouettes through his dark lashes. The animals stood in a row facing him, and he knew that they knew, that he was awake. As he opened his eyes, he noticed that each of them was staring at him. He averted their gaze, then cautiously glanced at them and felt as though they were waiting for him to address them. "I guess I owe someone here a thank you for getting me out of the fire."

"You thank, Ellie," said O.

"Thank you, Ellie," Jabari said with a firm nod.

Ellie lowered her trunk. "You saved my life first. It was the least I could do." The soft voice from such a large creature surprised Jabari.

"You saved all our lives," said Lefu.

The zebra nodded. "Agreed."

O gazed at Jabari. "Thank you, Jabari. We all owe you life."

A breeze blew over the forest, carrying with it the scent of smoke from the charred circus, and a somber silence settled over them as they contrasted their fate with those who'd been trapped in their cages.

"Now, where were we?" said Z after what he felt was an awkward eternity.

"You said… we need… a plan," said Jabari, still unsettled that he could speak with them.

"Yes, yes," Z continued, elevating his voice while eyeing Lefu. "I propose that we return promptly to the circus grounds and make ourselves known and be returned to our stations post haste… I am not a deserter."

Lefu growled: "Are you crazy? You *want* to go back!"

Z lifted his head high and spoke with an authoritative voice. "I am a professional, and I take my work seriously. The honorable thing to do is return."

"What are we supposed to return to?" said Lefu. "The circus is gone. The tent, the trailers, the food; it's all gone!"

Z pushed out his chest, "Surely the Malcolm brothers will be there to salvage what they can. Surely, they will be delighted to see us. We can start over and help them rebuild. After all, we are the stars of the show, aren't we?" Z was sure of himself, that his logic was flawless, and that he'd won them over.

Lefu snarled. "I'll die before going back," then gazed into the woods in the direction of the smoke.

Z's eyes widened at Lefu's grave emphasis on "die," and he

turned to the elephant. "Ellie, you of all of us know we can't survive without the circus. You need food—a *lot* of food, and *they* can get it for you." The zebra pointed his head toward the former circus, "Besides, we aren't safe here by ourselves." Z looked at Ellie, waiting for a response, when O added his weight to the unbalanced discussion:

"You very sure… why you want us to go with you?" Z held his head high and looked down at O, as if he were speaking to a child. "Isn't it obvious… you're going to die out here! You'll either be shot or starve, but you simply can't make it on your own,".

"Thank you," said O, his large, clear eyes watching Z with a penetrating gaze.

Z's nostrils flared. He raised his now agitated voice, "I can't believe you don't get it. We were made for the circus, and the circus was made for us. We don't belong out here by ourselves."

O glanced at Z. "You right, we no belong alone."

Z seized the moment to leverage the lore of the orangutan's wisdom. "Even O agrees!"

O raised a long, hairy finger as he spoke. "I not say belong in circus. I say we no be alone."

Z looked as if he didn't comprehend the difference, which wasn't unique: many animals in the circus didn't understand O. To driven creatures like Z, O was an enigma. He showed no ambition, no drive, no guts, and no power; he was everything Z was not. To him, O appeared weak and old with nothing to offer. Z most often referred to animals like O as AWC—a cruel acronym that stood for *a wasted cage*.

The only life Z understood was performing, and the jury of his mind convicted anyone who didn't give as much as him. He was proud of himself and his place in the circus. This was more than personal truth for Z: it was universal truth, and many in the traveling group shared his view—especially those that suffered the least.

Z saw in the moonlit faces of the others that they didn't share his feelings, and the thought of returning. He suspected they'd experienced more pain at the hands of others, but he always thought he'd done what they were not willing to do. He had a 'buck up' attitude. In his mind, he, too, had borne difficulties, but he thought he'd sacrificed to overcome them to become a respected performer and team member. Though never stating it, he felt superior.

After a long moment of hopeful staring, he gave a disgusted shake of his head. He then turned and, with his nose held high, marched out of the clearing toward the smell of burnt wood.

THREE

Zebras by nature are cautious herd animals, and Z was no exception. In a group he was confident, but alone, approaching this unknown situation, he was unsure of himself. As he walked through the woods toward the field behind the former tent, he pondered what might happen to him if he were to walk out in the open. He feared he'd be shot, or even captured by someone he didn't know. *I must get to familiar faces… but a zebra on the loose will certainly draw attention.*

With that thought, he halted, turned back and walked to a narrow trail leading to a mud bog that he'd passed on his way back from standing guard. After exploring the depth of the mud with one hoof, he then committed the second. Confident he wouldn't get sucked into the center of the earth, he rolled into the muck and twisted and turned in the sticky slop, until thick black mud slathered him from mane to hoof. *A zebra without his stripes is just a common horse,* he prided himself.

Z worked his way out of the mud hole and stood. He noticed that the moisture in the bog appeared to trickle in from a nearby water source. With nothing to drink since the evening prior, he followed the moist ground, and it led him to a clearing containing a large oval pond with wide, flat banks of grass, surrounded by trees, shrubs and taller grasses. He instinctively studied the perimeter for predators. Satisfied that he was safe and alone, he approached the still waters and spread his front legs, lowering his mouth to take a much-needed drink. He extended his tongue but hesitated when he saw his reflection in the moonlit water.

Z was adept at many things but being relaxed was not one of them. He believed that zebras had a job to do and a reputation to uphold, and Z was nothing if not a good zebra. He labored his entire life to earn and sustain respect, and it left little room for relaxing. Yes, he occasionally did relaxed things, but he never fully let go. On guard and ever vigilant, he never stopped being his duty-bound self—determined to never sully his respectable image.

But when he saw the creature reflected in the pond, it shocked him, yet for a reason not understood, it gave him a lightness that he couldn't place. He tilted his head left and then right, surveying himself for a hint of zebra, and not finding any, he became titillated at the prospect of being something else. Believing the power of the costume he now wore, it gave him the courage to lower his guard for the first time, in many, many, years.

Pretending to be the horse he now appeared to be, he first trotted, which soon became an outright gallop of excitement. He ran as fast as he could around the pond, but soon remembered his stripes hiding under the mud and came to an abrupt stop. He looked around, confirmed that he was still alone, and dropped his head to chastise himself. *What are you doing? This isn't how a zebra conducts himself.*

With his head bowed in shame, he turned to leave the pond when he glimpsed his blackened front legs. Though he'd just tried to convince himself how zebras shouldn't behave, seeing himself covered in mud was a contradiction his logical mind couldn't dismiss. He was a complete mess, looking nothing like the proud zebra he thought himself to be. So much so, he burst into braying laughter which loosened something within him, and he resumed his charge. Head held back, he augmented his galloping and weaving by interspersing it with prancing and trotting. He not only forgot he was a zebra, he forgot everything as the moment consumed him, and he played with abandon in the moonlit reflections on the surface of the pond.

    Deeply satisfied, he came to a stop, unable to contain the smile that spread across his face—his teeth exposed in an endearing gummy beam. At first, he couldn't remember the last time he'd smiled so broadly or felt so happy. In all his years of training, and all its rewards, he calculated that nothing had ever paid him so dearly. He also recalled laughing with others, and at others, but this was different. This didn't come from the same place and certainly didn't feel the same—it only looked that way. It struck him that he'd felt like this as a colt, before he became part of the circus. "Useless" feelings as he used to describe them—feelings covered over by responsibilities and a reputation to garner.

    This is how I felt when I ran freely in the savannah as a colt, he thought to himself, now sure that he recognized the emotion. While the soft breeze evaporated his sweat through the layer of mud, he closed his eyes and allowed the surge of emotion to blend with his childhood memory. He recalled long forgotten days of unbridled fun under blue African skies. Days of wonder and joy. Days of freedom from everything he now deemed so important. His heart glowed with warmth and happiness, and a rare pulse of emotion surged through his entire body as his eyes became moist.

FOUR

The light of dawn appeared in the eastern sky as Jabari, O, Ellie and Lefu walked through the cool, crisp morning on an old logging road, away from the circus grounds. The seldom-used road carved through the edge of the hills and had trees on either side, giving them a sense of safety as they walked. Years of wagons and caravans had compacted the earth in two narrow strips, but fresh greens filled the center between the tracks that delighted Ellie. The occasional tree also lured her, and she tore off bunches of green leaves, only to catch up moments later to not be too far from the group. Lefu took the lead—having a lion in front gave them a sense of protection—with Jabari and O walking behind him, one on each wheel path.

They walked in silence, taking in their newfound freedom. This was the first time in many years that the animals had experienced life without chains, cages, or whips. A new awareness overcame them as they absorbed every tree, cloud, and bird—as though seeing everything for the first time. Although they didn't know from where it came, they felt something very good deep inside. With every step of their feet, the earth spoke to their body, which subtly absorbed the message; the earth belonged to them, they to it, and it was their right to be free.

After a long stretch of silence, Ellie broke it with a simple question. It revealed the obvious problem that no one had yet dared raise. "Where are we going?" She delivered it with a nervous undertone that betrayed her insecurities.

Jabari stopped and turned to her and grimaced. "I don't

know." He kicked at the grass between the ruts of the road, then looked up at the treetops blowing in the wind, as if gauging their problems against their height. *Lost, alone, afraid, hungry, with no friends, shelter, or direction. What will become of us?* He let out a breath of despair. But as he looked past the trees, for the second time in as many days, he saw the now-fading stars, and although without a plan, he somehow felt hopeful.

FIVE

For hours, Z looked across the moonlit field from the shadow of the woods, searching for any sign of the Malcolm brothers near the remains from the fire. Circus performers arrived and left with dismay at the scene, some too drunk to comprehend the reality of what they saw. Others lingered, but there was no sign of the owners.

After his run around the pond, Z had an urge to rejoin the others, but he convinced himself otherwise. It returned in the early morning, but he resisted the feeling and decided again to listen his thoughts—rational, familiar thoughts that he could understand and justify. He'd felt emotions like this many times before, urging him to say or do something out of character, but he'd trained himself to fight them and push them aside. Although he did it again this night, he now found it more difficult than ever.

The sun rose and the morning passed into afternoon before his patience was rewarded. Malcolm Jr., dressed in his top hat, became visible in the distance, accompanied by his brother, and a third man in fine attire. This man reviewed the scene, sized up the situation with nods, and took notes in a large book. With little left of the circus, the exchange was brief, and with firm handshakes and a tip of Malcolm Jr.'s hat, the third man departed.

Z seized the moment. He ambled out of the woods and across the field, toward the circus grounds. The charred trailers formed a visual block which was both an advantage, and a disadvantage to Z—*to not see means not to be seen.* He thought to himself. He lost sight of the brothers as they moved behind one of the metal sided trailers and decided this might be his only chance. Determined to get back to safety and excited to be welcomed home, he darted to it. Standing behind it with his short tail twitching, he strained to hear voices on the other side. He turned and twisted his large ears until he caught the ringmaster's familiar tone.

Z put forward a hoof, then hesitated, remembering that if he walked out now covered in muck, they might not recognize him. He extended his head around the back edge of the trailer to scrape off the earth, when his keen ears heard Malcolm Jr. speaking in a hushed but boastful tone: "I told you it would work! We're out of this mess and getting top dollar and all it took was a quiet night and little fire.

The elder laughed. "I never thought insurance would be the best investment we ever made."

Z heard a pat on the back, followed by footsteps as they walked away from the trailer.

SIX

After walking most of the night and all day, Jabari, Ellie, O, and Lefu were thirsty, hungry, and exhausted. The sun was setting, and they'd come no closer to answer Ellie's question. As they rounded a corner, an old logging shed came into view. Supported by four tall posts, it was high enough for even Ellie to walk under. Though long out of use, the sawdust from many years of cutting covered the floor, making it a comfortable place to spend the night. The timing was opportune, as large raindrops fell, tinging on the corrugated metal roof. Rain flowed from the roof edge in narrow streams and the animals quenched their thirst as Jabari filled his canteen. They then laid down under the shelter to rest their tired feet, except Ellie who looked back from where they came, with her ears lifted high. "Someone's coming!"

Jabari shot up, eyes wide in panic. "What do you mean, someone's coming?"

Ellie looked down and concentrated on her feet. "It's a horse, approaching fast from where we came."

Fear set into them and they darted out of the structure to hide behind nearby trees. Ellie hid the furthest back to cover her size, joined by Lefu.

Images of an angry search party led by the Malcolm brothers ran through Jabari's mind. Although frightened, he was eager to see who was coming. Accompanied by O, Jabari positioned himself behind a few large trees close to the road and watched the bend in the trail for who it might reveal.

"How do you know someone's coming?" asked Lefu, as he

and Ellie waited in the darkness with their eyes barely visible to each other; one pair set high and wide, and the other low and close.

"I feel it with my feet."

"Are you sure about this?"

"Yes, of course. My feet are very sensitive. I can detect heavy movement from far distances. It's one of the ways we communicated at… home…" She trailed off, remembering better days as raindrops landed on them.

Ellie sensed something in his silence. "Don't you miss home?"

His silence confirmed her intuition, but she held her powerful tongue; *this isn't the time or place,* she thought.

SEVEN

Z's heart sank at the words of Malcolm Jr. and he became oblivious to his surroundings. He turned and walked back toward the forest in a daze, and upon reaching the cover of trees, brayed and kicked against the air, before starting an angry charge into the woods. How could they have done this! He thought to himself. I trusted them ... I gave my life to this! He didn't know where he was going, but he found himself on a trail, and galloped as fast as his powerful legs would take him.

As he ran, rain began to fall and rinsed the mud from his body, and he wished it were his feelings that were washing away—he felt more on this day than he had in many years combined and it reminded him why he'd worked so hard to avoid emotions. Driven by the anger of his betrayal, he had no idea how far he ran, or where he was, but as he rounded a corner, he heard his name, and slowed to a trot.

"Z is that you?" the voice repeated.

Z turned his head back and saw Jabari step out onto the trail from behind a tree, with the old orangutan to his side, both dripping wet.

"What happened? What are you doing here?" asked Jabari.

Z stopped and stared at them and they sensed this was not the same confident creature that had left them that morning.

O elevated his long arm in the logging shed's direction, then turned toward it. "Shelter."

Z followed O with his head low and eyes to the ground. He gave a quick "Thank you." between panting breaths as they walked to the shelter.

Ellie and Lefu observed the exchange, and with their curiosity aroused, they hurried back, eager to learn why Z returned.

EIGHT

Rain cooled the night air, and Jabari gathered wood scraps from years of lumber cutting, along with dry grass from the edges inside the roofline. He had no possessions, save the few things he carried with him: a canteen around his neck and a satchel that hung from his shoulder under his tan jacket, which held his savings and a few coveted personal items. A pouch on his belt held a knife and flint, which he struck together toward the pile of dry grass, until sparks leaped onto the kindling. He cupped his hands around the grass and puffed gently. After several breaths, the sparks transformed into smoke, and then into small flames that burned the grass. Jabari added the wood and soon fire illuminated their faces. They circled around to absorb the warmth and dry their bodies.

Ellie shook her ears, splashing water as she entered the shelter. "Are you okay, Z—you don't look well?"

Z's companions looked at one another with concern as Z lost himself in the fire. "...They burned down the circus."

"Who burned down the circus?" Lefu asked with a growl.

Z's white stripes danced in the fire. "The Malcom brothers."

"What!" said Ellie.

Jabari raised his eyebrows. "What do you mean, they burned it down?"

"I mean they burned it down for 'insurance'."

Lefu growled a low rumble. "What are you talking about?"

Z's nostrils flared and he blew out hard. "I heard them talking when I got to them. They wanted out, and they burned it down to get 'insurance money.' It was the younger brother's plan!"

Ellie gasped. "The Ring Master!"

Z, now having their understanding, hung his head low. "Yes."

Stillness fell over the group as they took in what Z had carried alone until then.

Tears welled in Ellie's eyes as she remembered those she knew and loved. "They killed all those animals."

Lefu growled. "You mean they tried to kill us!"

"I can't believe it… it can't be true." blubbered Ellie.

Jabari nodded. "Now it makes sense… the brothers were there the night of the fire, long after everyone left. I saw them before I fell asleep and woke up to the fire. Z's telling the truth." Jabari's eyes met Z's.

Ellie halted her sobbing. "How could they do such a thing?"

The question remained in the air for a moment before Z spoke again, his eyes angry and fixed on the fire. "I gave my life to their circus!"

Lefu roared: "If I ever see them again, I'll kill them!"

Ellie cried again.

O moved toward her, placed his right hand on her forehead between her eyes, and gently wiped away a tear with his other hand. Her breathing became softer, and she ceased crying. He then patted her a few times. "No control over circus… only how react."

Exhausted from their travels and heavy from Z's news, they made ready for sleep, as the sound of raindrops danced overhead.

Jabari leaned over and whispered to O, "What did you mean by what you said to Ellie?"

"What you think?" said O.

"I think you meant that we're helpless and can only hope to keep calm."

O hesitated with his eyes fixed on the tin ceiling. "…Sleep

now; talk tomorrow."
	"Good night," said Jabari.
	"Good night," said O.
	A few moments passed, then Jabari whispered, "I'm glad we can now talk with each other." He then rolled over and fell asleep.

NINE

Z

The floodlights twisted and circled, spinning on their pivots from the ceiling of the great tent. Their operator drew the crowd's attention to the center and largest of the three rings, under the cavernous structure. The lights panned across the dirt floor, then up and down the rows of people, giving Z—who waited just outside the rear entrance—a glimpse of the crowd anticipating his performance. Like a soldier awaiting his commanding officer's direction, Z was ready to perform.

The orchestra music began. His entry was timed to the third clang of the cymbal early in the music. His trainer snapped his whip, and Z pranced through the tent entrance and out onto the ring. *Like clockwork,* he praised himself. The music softened and the ringmaster introduced the act from the coned-shaped megaphone. The lights brightened, and the crowd grew excited, chattering at the sight of the zebra with his striking black and white stripes, as he pranced around the outside edge of the center ring.

After completing the full circumference of the circle so the entire audience saw his unique beauty, the whip snapped again, accompanied by a command. Z accelerated his pace from prancing, to a brisk trot. At the same time as the whip hit the dirt floor, two clowns carried a fence jumping obstacle into the ring behind the zebra, followed by more clowns bringing two more jumps of greater height, setting them up with increasing distances apart.

Z knew the routine well, but more than that, he prided himself on the quality of his performance. This was his life, and the circus was serious business. He paced his steps with great precision as all his faculties focused on the routine; as often as he'd done it, he always delivered.

He approached the first jump and without hesitation, fluidly leaped over it. The noise of the crowd's applause flowed after him. After only a few more paces, again without delay or a break in his stride, he leaped over the second obstacle, and again the crowd applauded. As he approached the third obstacle, something within distracted him, but he didn't take the opportunity to identify it—*focus Z, focus,* he chastised himself. *Concentrate*! He thrust his front legs up into the air and powered down with his hind legs to project himself up and over the last jump. To his disbelief and astonishment, he felt and heard the crack of his knee collide with the top fence bar, knocking it off its supports. A second later, the crowd heard it, and a second later, he heard the crowd. In that moment, Z experienced something that only happened to others—to undisciplined animals who didn't take their work seriously—performers who weren't willing to sacrifice and pay the price he had.

With his momentum broken, gravity pulled him downward. His knees hit the ground first, followed hard by his chest and neck skidding into the earth. Brown dirt plowed under his chin and flew into the air on either side of him. As the dust rose, so did his hind legs, high into the air, taking with them his back, forcing his head sideways, with his chin pressed hard into the ground. Driven with inertia, his body flipped over him and slammed him hard onto his back, driving out his breath in a thud, that even the furthest seats could hear in the now silent arena. His lungs wheezed trying to re-capture their lost breath. Covered in dirt with his legs flailing, he rolled onto his side. The dust settled, revealing the crowd to him as inner voices screamed words of judgement and condemnation. In a disoriented emotional blur, the proud zebra struggled to stand. Trying to escape his humiliation, he scraped the ground at his side to gain a footing, but the weight of his shame was too heavy.

Z awoke lying on his side, kicking his powerful legs. Drenched in sweat, his heart pounded, and his blood coursed with anxiety. He looked around and realized that he was not performing but lying under the tin roof of the shelter.

He knew the dream well and it always ended at the same moment. As the fog of sleep left him, details of the dream vaporized. Although he tried to push it out, he could still feel the shame of his imagined failure.

He had long understood himself enough to know that fear drove him at some level, but he only knew this intellectually—he never allowed himself to *feel* his fear. This he'd kept under control and repressed. It had propelled him to his place of prominence amongst his peers, but he was unaware how deeply it went. For many years he'd been content with this knowledge and the results. It had worked well for him, and he'd garnered a reputation as a no-nonsense, hardworking soldier who'd earned his stripes; always reliable, always eager, always perfect, always, always, always… but this dream troubled Z.

He couldn't tell if the dreams caused him to think more about his fear, or if thinking more about the fear, caused the dreams to come in greater frequency. Regardless, like the jumps in his dream, his fear came with ever increasing regularity and intensity, and it was getting harder and harder to overcome. Not only was he now aware of his fear, but he was terrified that he couldn't control it. He saw no relief from this vicious circle: The more he thought about it, the more anxious he became, and the more afraid he became, the more he dreamed it. The very thing that drove him to take control, now threatened to control him.

He also couldn't understand why, after having achieved his measure of success after all these years, was he still afraid? This question began as a hairline crack in his hard-set mind but eroded into a well-defined fissure. This troubled him because he believed he was in control and that he charted his own destiny by the strength of his will.

    Z soothed himself by nudging his nose on the ground and tried to recall what distracted him as he approached the third jump. Try as he may in recent months, he couldn't place the murky emotion that lingered in his body when he awoke from the nightmare. He sensed that if he could recall the distraction in the dream right before his last jump, he'd have the key to releasing his anxiety and fear.

TEN

Jabari stirred and lifted his head, looking around with half-shut eyes. The zebra was standing and chomping grasses. The lion was under the shelter flipping his tail from side to side, while the elephant was pulling leaves from a nearby tree. The orangutan was nowhere to be seen.

Jabari stretched his arms over his head. "Where's O?"

Lefu licked a paw. "Z was the first one up."

Z heard his name and looked at Jabari. "He wasn't here when I woke up."

Jabari sat up and hunger pained him, and he thought about Lefu's food disadvantage. "How are you holding up, Lefu."

"Hungry."

Jabari nodded. "Me too."

Until waking up this morning, Jabari had never felt responsible for anything or anyone, other than himself. Not that he was selfish. In fact, he was quite ordinary for his young age. He thought a great deal about his future hopes and dreams —love for a girl, a home and a family—aspects of a life not yet lived. But this morning, he felt responsible for these animals. Not guilt, nor a burden of responsibility, but a clarity that this was his path, though he was completely unsure of what to do next. He knew he could leave, but to do so would be to walk away from what he sensed was something bigger than himself. How he felt when he saved them, and more so, how he could now speak with them, made it clear that this was his destiny, even if he didn't know where it would take him.

Jabari leaned toward Lefu. "I'm going to get us some food."

Ellie's eyes widened and she pointed with her trunk. "There's a village down there. I saw it this morning from a pond I found by the ridge." She motioned with her trunk again, excited by her discoveries.

"Thanks, Ellie!"

Jabari stood, rubbed his still-tired eyes and walked down the sloped path in the direction Ellie's trunk had pointed. Out of sight from the others, O appeared as if out of nowhere, and accompanied him. "Walk with?"

Jabari jumped in surprise but was glad to have company. "Yes, of course!"

"Where go?"

Jabari pointed down the hill. "To town, for food."

"So, you stay with us then?"

Jabari grimaced. "Um… Yeah."

"Then you understand what I say yesterday."

Jabari furrowed his brow, "I don't think so… you said that we can't control what happens to us, only how we respond."

O focused on Jabari. "You understand but don't know yet."

Jabari raised an eyebrow.

O smiled knowingly at him. "You no resist. You no complain. You no run. You no blame. You accept."

"Oh, I blame the Malcolm brothers!"

O lifted his arm overhead and scratched his back, with his elbow bobbing as he walked. "Yes, they responsible… but you help now?"

Jabari shrugged. "I guess so… how couldn't I? Besides, what good would those things do, anyway?"

O waddled from side to side next to him on the path. "Most not learn to accept hard things. They run. They hide. They complain. They miss gift."

Jabari studied O, struggling to take in what the orangutan was saying when O placed his hand on Jabari's shoulder. "To accept opens door to meaning of life," said O.

O was silent for a few steps, allowing Jabari to take in his words before he continued, gravely. "You be tested again… maybe when more to lose?"

    Jabari's skin tingled as goosebumps covered his arms; he knew there was truth in O's words. He lifted his head and saw the road was in clear view for a long distance and realized they were now visible to anyone approaching on the same path. Jabari turned to his companion. "You probably shouldn't go any further." Jabari then realized he was once again, walking alone.

ELEVEN

The old logging road ended without fanfare at a T. One arm headed in the direction of the city that had drawn the circus crowds, while the other continued to the town Ellie had pointed out. The road was narrow and lined with trees; their rustling leaves accompanied by the songs of nightingales that drew out Jabari's voice, singing with them as he strolled.

After exhausting his repertoire, Jabari found himself in the small village that had several shops, including a grocer opposite a cafe. He made his way to the store and collected what he thought would satisfy everyone: meat for Lefu; vegetables and fruit for himself, O, and Ellie, and a bag of oats for Z. He filled his canteen from the fountain and after taking a much-needed drink, he approached the checkout. The shopkeeper eyed Jabari. "You new around here?"

Jabari shuffled. "Just passing through."

The clerk eyed the goods as he tallied them. "That's quite an order."

Jabari shifted the conversation. "How far is it to Port City?"

"About 20 miles," said the man as he punched another item into the register.

Jabari gave a wide smile. "This should do it then!"

The man announced the total and Jabari reached into his satchel to pay, then hesitated, realizing that home was now further away than ever. The merchant held his hand out and

Jabari's face sank as he paid him.

The man returned Jabari a few small coins. "…and your change."

Jabari placed the coins in his satchel and closed it. "Thank you."

With several bags in each hand he exited the store. As he walked back, he noticed a man sitting on the café patio, who appeared to be watching him. Jabari thought he recognized him but did not want to draw attention to himself and looked away.

After the lengthy walk from town, the return climb up the hill was difficult with the heat of the now-higher sun, the weight of the heavy bags of food, and a full canteen. He stopped to rest several times along the way, and each time he paused, he sensed that someone was following him. He couldn't make out who it was, but when he turned to look, he thought he saw, from the corner of his eye, someone darting out of view behind the cover of trees. A vein in his neck began pulse—this time he was sure. He collected his thoughts, ensured his satchel was hidden under his vest, and that his knife was in its pouch on his belt. He then picked up his bags and walked on, until he rounded a bend in the path, whereupon he ran as fast as he could. When he spotted what he was looking for, he darted into the woods.

TWELVE

Sultan and the lion

The lion tamer stepped into place to ready himself for his introduction. He stood in the darkness, long whip in hand, coiled and ready at his side. He was short, olive-skinned with short arms and his wide black mustache underlined bony cheekbones under dark brown eyes. He wore a brown cloth head wrap, with a decorative golden pin on the front that held it in place over his thin, oily black hair. His tan jacket had long, loose sleeves; a high collar covered in geometric embroidery; small, ivory colored buttons from the waist to the neck, and gold piping that matched the color of his pants. These were airy, and tied off at the ankle, above jeweled shoes, that came to a point beyond the toes and curled backwards, wilting over the laces. He called himself Sultan the Great, though he was neither.

"Ladies and gentlemen," said the ringmaster, preparing the crowd for the next show. "Now, in the center ring… the amazing, the death defying… Sultan the Great… lion tamer!"

"The Great Sultan my @%#^!" Lefu muttered, matching and mocking the ring-masters tone. "I'll give you a show you'll never forget—watch me tear him to pieces and see what they think of their Sultan then!"

Every performance began this way, and Lefu was sure it would be his last. Or at least Sultan's last, if Lefu were to somehow escape certain execution.

The tent lights beamed onto the center ring, illuminating

the lion cage that was discreetly assembled in the shadows during a distracting clown performance on the other side of the tent. With a commanding yell, Sultan cracked his whip and the thunder of the majestic lion bellowed over the crowd. The sound reverberated from deep and low within the beast, causing the hair on everyone's neck to stand up. The primal reaction enslaved the mammalian brain, and all eyes fixed on Lefu.

He was a sight to behold, and the on-lookers gasped in awe, wonder, or fear. His majesty was brilliant; it radiated from his golden mane that crowned him the true king that he was. Taller than any man when he stood on his hind legs, his size and stature were imposing. His razor-sharp claws, the length of a finger, could effortlessly disembowel a foe, while his dagger-like fangs glistened in the spotlight as he stretched his muscular neck to release the bellows of anger, driving out yet another seething roar.

Despite his rage over the years, Lefu had learned to cope with his pain:

I'm alive and fed.
I have a roof over my head.
I'm not dead.

Like a childhood rhyme, he used his incantations when the humiliation of performing plagued him; comfort for the shame of being whipped into obedience by a half-wit drunk, with a made-up name. This Sultan took credit for what he neither created nor owned: he only dominated Lefu through the power of captivity. The lion-tamer had no respect or reverence for the magnificent creature that Lefu was. He only feared the harm he could do—not relevant to the splendid creature itself, but only relative to his own personal risk. Lefu was more than angry, and Sultan did not know how close he was to experiencing the wrath of a king dethroned.

Sultan ran through the routine that had changed little in the years since Lefu was part of the performing pride. Roars, followed by jumps, leading to feigned clawing at the whip—as though to convince the crowd that Sultan's death was imminent.

If only Sultan knew …

He was very young when he'd first started, and never imagined he'd still be where he was today—performing the same tricks—more growls and roars, followed by yet more jumps and positioning, ending with Sultan's head in Lefu's mouth.

If only Sultan knew…

THIRTEEN

From Jabari's vantage point in the tree he'd climbed, he confirmed that he was being followed; the pursuer peeked around the corner and slowed from a run, back to a cautious walk. He looked ahead and realized he'd lost his quarry, then ran on hoping to catch up. He soon gave up and slunk down, winded, at the bottom of the very tree Jabari was hiding in. The man withdrew a flask from his vest and took a swig.

Jabari planned to remain until the man left, but as he waited, it appeared to him that the man was crying. Jabari's fear diminished and his anger rose. "Why are you following me!"

Startled, the man wiped his face and gathered himself. With his flask in hand, he looked around, then up. Jabari's eyes tightened. "I know you... you're... Sultan the Lion Tamer!"

The man looked up and saw Jabari. "It is you!" said the man in a smooth Spanish accent.

Jabari's eyes went fiery. "Why are you following me!"

"You haven't heard?" said the man with an air of intrigue.

Curious, Jabari shifted his weight to come more into view. "Heard what?"

Sultan took a sip from his flask. "The word is that you burned down the circus... people are looking for you."

Jabari's mouth dropped and his eyes bulged. "What!"

Sultan waved his index finger at Jabari. "You were the only one not at the celebration, and you were gone when the first of us came back…"

Jabari narrowed his eyes in righteous anger. "I had nothing to do with it. I would never hurt those animals!"

Sultan twisted his body and looked up, eying Jabari for a long moment, weighing his words. He maintained eye contact and asked, "What are you doing here then?"

Jabari hesitated and fell silent. He felt foolish for having confronted his follower while stuck in the tree above him. He was also angry for being accused of burning down the circus. "You wouldn't understand."

"Try me, amigo."

The man's sympathetic tone gave Jabari hope. He looked up, and realizing he had nothing to lose, looked below and told Sultan what happened the night of the fire. He told them about the Malcom Brothers at the tent; falling asleep and waking up; the animals he saved; that he didn't know what else to do, and didn't want the animals to be hurt, or taken to face an uncertain fate.

Sultan sat at the bottom of the tree and waited until Jabari finished. "You, my friend, will need some help."

Jabari's eyes widened in surprise before doubt overtook his face. "What makes you think I trust you?"

"It looks to me like you need all the help you can get. Besides, if I wanted to harm you, I could report your location to people who might think differently than I do."

Jabari raised an eyebrow. "…Differently than you?"

"I happen to believe you… Jabari, isn't it?"

Jabari's body relaxed, and he climbed out of the tree. When he got to the bottom, the man was resting against the trunk, flask in one hand, the other extended. "I never used my real name in the circus—I'm Vicente."

FOURTEEN

After Jabari left for town, Ellie returned to forage on the trees by the pond, higher toward the ridge, leaving Z and Lefu alone together for the first time. Z grazed on grasses, while Lefu licked his paws, trying to keep his mind from his hunger. He decided conversation would be more effective, and lay his chin on his front paws, and looked toward Z. "What were you dreaming about this morning?"

Z's eyes froze for a fleeting moment, but the hesitation was captured by the great hunter.

"Nothing, just a little dream."

Lefu grinned. "That was no small dream. You were flailing and kicking and braying."

Z ignored the comment and returned to his grazing but Lefu forced the conversation. "You weren't the first one up this morning," he delivered flatly.

Z wasn't given to exposing himself, but with the events of the last few days, it somehow seemed to make sense. He stopped grazing and lifted his head and stared into the forest with a lost look in his eyes. "It's a dream I keep having over and over again. I can't figure it out."

"What's it about?"

Lefu's open tone surprised the zebra and he went on to explain the dream in detail. "Any idea what makes me hesitate before the jump?"

"Not a clue." said Lefu glibly to Z's dismay.

Lefu saw the zebra's agitation. "I'm sorry. I shouldn't have been so trite. What I mean is, I really don't know… I'm not very good at this kind of thing, but…" He hesitated for emphasis. "…I know someone who is."

Z appeared calm once again and took the hook that Lefu put forward. "Who… would that be?"

"O." Lefu watched Z's subtle eye movements and saw no judgement. Satisfied that Z was open, he continued. "He might not be very useful the way the likes of you see him, but it's the things you can't see that he's really good at."

Z held Lefu's gaze for a moment, then looked back to the forest to consider the advice, as Lefu headed to the ridge toward Ellie.

FIFTEEN

Jabari grabbed Vicente's hand and pulled him up. "I never trusted those Malcolm brothers." Jabari nodded in agreement. Vicente glanced at the bags behind the tree and Jabari's eyes narrowed. "How do I know I can trust you?"

Vicente turned and looked at Jabari. He placed one hand against the tree and held the other open, extended from his side. "Like I said before, you don't, but if you must know, like you, I have nothing to lose."

"What does that mean?" said Jabari.

"It means I lost everything in that fire, too. I have no home, no family, and no job." He grimaced and rotated his wrist, twisting his flask from side to side, sloshing its contents. "This is all I have left." Understanding loneliness, Jabari pursed his lips and nodded.

Vicente unscrewed the cap of his flask. "But when I saw you in town, something compelled me to follow you..." Vicente took a swig. "...It's strange to lose everything, only to discover you really didn't have anything at all."

Jabari raised an eyebrow. "Why do you want to help me?"

Vicente swallowed hard and cocked his head. "Because I really need to do something..." He searched for the right word for a moment. "...something good."

Jabari wrinkled his nose and Vicente saw his confusion. "I can only tell you that letting me help you would be a great favor to me."

Despite his reservations, Jabari felt Vicente's sincerity and a rush of excitement passed through him at the prospect of help. He snapped up a few of the bags. "This way." He walked off, leaving Vicente to collect the rest and catch up.

"So, what made you join the circus?" asked Jabari when Vicente caught up to him.

"I just sort of fell into it. I needed a job when the circus came to town and thought the travel would be exciting…" Vicente paused and glanced at Jabari. "…Got hired to do what you were doing."

Jabari's eyes widened at the correlation.

"So, the lion tamer took a liking to me and showed me how to work with the cats. Before long—" Vicente made a whipping gesture as he spoke. "—I was helping him in the shows. I liked the excitement and danger of it all. Then one day, he doesn't show for practice, and when I find him, he's face-down in his trailer—dead. Vicente's face drew slack. "…That really shook me up…Anyway, the Malcolm Brothers asked if I could do the show, and without thinking, I said, 'Si,' and that was that. I was the new Sultan the Great!" Vicente gave a bow and they laughed together at his theatrics for a moment, when Vicente tilted his head. "What animals did you say you saved?"

Jabari smiled as he listed them. "Ellie the Elephant, O the orangutan, Z, and Lefu, your lion."

"You have Lefu! It'll be great to see him again!" Vicente rubbed his chin. "Not exactly animals you can hide. Any ideas on how to get them somewhere safe?"

"I was hoping you might help; where *can* we go?"

"Where do they belong?" asked Vicente.

Jabari shrugged. "Home."

"What do you mean, home?"

"Except for O, it's where I'm from… the great savannah plains of Africa."

Vicente held his shoulders back and nodded, gradually. "…Well, then, Africa it is!"

Jabari's mouth dropped. Vicente said it like it was a decision he made every day—as if taking the animals to Africa was no greater effort than to cross the street. Jabari wondered if the drink was affecting him. "How are we going to do *that*?"

"It just so happens I have a friend in Port City. He's a boat captain who owes me a favor."

Jabari's eyes widened. "A boat?"

"Yes, a boat. Did you think we could *walk* there?"

Vicente's ideas raced through Jabari's mind, and he was doing his best to keep up.

Vicente tilted his head and looked up in thought. "How far is it to Port City from here?"

"20 miles," came Jabari's quick reply.

Vicente counted on his fingers with his thumb. "...Si, Si... it'll take us several days to get there...We'll have to figure a way to get them to Port City, but if we can, I think I can get you a ride."

Jabari had stuffed the hope of returning home into a deep place in his heart, but it now surged to the front of his chest. His entire body followed, and he thrust forward in excitement and he continued his climb with a broad smile on his face.

SIXTEEN

Z's grazing had a predictable pattern which included built-in safeguards: Lift head, look forward, look right, look left, return to center, hesitate, graze, repeat. He'd performed his ritual at least a hundred times this morning. But when he raised his head this time, he saw the orangutan descend from a tree by the pond, hanging from it with his left foot, while holding a fruit in his right hand. As he touched the ground with his left hand, his left foot released from the branch, and he somersaulted, landing in a seated position, hair askew, looking straight at Z.

Z continued grazing, and it took him a long time to get within a reasonable distance of O, to begin a conversation. When he arrived, the orangutan sat at the base of the tree with bits of apple laying in the grass next to him.

Z's soldier-self had deserted him the night before and had not returned. "...Good... morning."

O gazed at the four-legged creature before him.

Z continued with another grazing pattern, then raised his head. "Do you mind if I ask you a question?" Speaking with a creature he hadn't acknowledged before, he added, "...Lefu said you might be able to help me."

O scratched his back with satisfaction. "About dream?"

"Yeah... how did you know?"

O pointed up at the tree he came from. "Above you in morning. Hear you and lion talk." The orangutan sprawled himself out on the grass. "You no look up much," but the double meaning was lost on the zebra.

"Then you know what I want to know...can you tell me what I ask myself in the dream before the last jump?"

The orangutan sat up and grasped a branch and effortlessly lifted himself with one hand, raising his feet off the ground. He hung from it casually for a few moments before he responded. "Question we ask before all big jump. Sometime question test strength when we do what we should. Sometime question to change when not."

Z gazed at him.

O's body twisted side to side as the branch strained with his weight. "Question is why you do what you do, why you jump at all? Question we must all ask. Sometime often."

"But... I know why I'm jumping."

"You know why you jump on outside..." O pointed to his stomach with his free hand. "...but why you jump on *inside*?"

O's ears retreated and his lips went tight. He thought for a few moments and as he pondered O's words, he felt them—as though they were trying to reach something within. He was about to choke the emotion and focus his thoughts but decided instead to let go and see what these words were trying to touch.

O watched Z consider his counsel for too long and came to his aide. "Not easy to be herd animal."

Z recalled his early days in the circus, when he was introduced to the performing zebras as a colt. He remembered how he felt when they teased him, when he was anything other than strong and confident. He yearned to be accepted as one of them and became determined to fit in—at any cost.

"What design you have on body?" asked O, interrupting Z's thoughts.

Z sniffed. "Stripes."

O let go of the branch and sat on the ground. He drew a line in the dirt next to him. "What be you if have no stripes?"

Z thought for a moment. "I don't know."

O drew another line in the earth next to the first. "So, you need stripes to be zebra?"

"I guess so," answered Z with a half snort, unsure where the discussion was going.

"Would you be zebra if only have one stripe?"

Z hesitated, then chuckled. "Sure, but a strange one."

O looked up from the lines he had drawn and stared at Z. "Then be stripe you are…like you the only stripe…Even if strange."

Z glanced at O and back at the lines in the dirt and connected his past with his present. The message landed as gently as a feather. It was as if he'd known all along but was finally ready to listen. *Rejection.* As the word contacted its target, Z embraced it, and a knowing and relieved smile formed on his face. "I'm afraid of being rejected," he reported to O, as much as to himself.

O reached up for the branch above him and lifted himself up again.

Like a long held lie confessed, Z's burden of anxiety lifted. He raised his head and looked at O again, but this time with gratitude and… something more; for the first time, he respected the strange creature hanging in front of him.

SEVENTEEN

Ellie tore small branches from the trees on the ridge and spoke between mouthfuls. "Do you think we'll ever get home?"

Lefu protracted his claws and scratched at the ground. "No idea."

"Don't you want to go home some day?"

Lefu scratched at the ground again. "I've done everything I can to put that place out of my mind. I don't even want to think about it. Anyway, we aren't going home, so what does it matter?"

Ellie paused her grazing and looked at him with kindness in her eyes. "What is it about going home that causes you so much pain?"

Lefu shifted his weight then stood up. "I don't wanna talk about it."

Ellie narrowed her eyes. "You know you aren't the only one feeling pain."

Lefu glared at her—few dared to speak so directly to him.

She ignored his stare. "Everyone in the circus feels pain, Lefu. We didn't choose what happened to us, but we can choose what we do with our pain... but it takes courage."

Her words hit Lefu in multiple places at once: they stung his pride as he was sure he was no coward; they rubbed his unhealed wound, and he was afraid, though little of this he could acknowledge. It was too much for Lefu and he resorted to what had always worked; he turned his head and roared angry insults, then walked down the hill toward the shelter.

Ellie's body shrank, and a flush of fear and shame shot through her. She wasn't afraid of Lefu, and although she saw his anger coming, her response to reproach always took her by surprise. As hard as she'd tried to unravel them, her tangled emotions confounded her; she couldn't overcome her need for acceptance.

EIGHTEEN

The late morning sun was in full force by the time Jabari and Vicente reached the last section of the old logging road. Jabari paused, wiped sweat from his forehead and turned to Vicente. "The animals are around this corner. Let me go ahead before I bring you to them—I... don't want to scare them."

Winded, Vicente gladly accepted with a quick "Okay" and a nod and sat on a fallen tree near the edge of the road and caught his breath.

Jabari set down his supplies, then made his way up the road and disappeared around the corner.

When he arrived at the shelter, he found Z and O enjoying its shade, and Lefu walking from the forest into the clearing. "Where's Ellie," he asked the group.

"Up the hill," came Lefu's terse response.

"I need her; can you get her?" Jabari asked in a tone that would accept no argument.

Lefu grumbled under his breath and bared a few teeth, then turned and walked up the hill. A few minutes later, he returned and joined the group beneath the shelter. Ellie trailed behind.

Jabari glanced over his shoulder to be sure Vicente hadn't followed. "I have some exciting news. I met someone in the village who can help us get home!"

"Home?" said Z.

"What do you mean home?" Ellie asked.

"I mean *Africa* home."

"What are you talking about?" Lefu growled. "How are we going to get home?"

"I met a man on the way from town, and I explained my… our situation, and… he offered to help us. Anyway, he has a friend who has a boat who owes him a favor, and if we can make it to Port City, we can get back home."

Ellie squinted. "Why is he offering to help us?"

Jabari twisted his mouth, unsure how to explain what had just transpired. He decided it would be easier to sum things up. "He wants to help. Like us, he lost everything. I trust him… we have no one else. What do you think?" Jabari looked at them, one at a time.

Z planted a hoof firmly. "I vote yes," taking the group by surprise.

"You mean you're going to trust this stranger with our lives!" growled Lefu.

"I'm in," said Ellie.

Jabari's eyes settled on O. "I know Africa isn't your home, but you could live with me."

O smiled with his eyes. "I travel with."

"That leaves you, Lefu," said Z, as the group awaited his response.

"I want to meet him first," Lefu said with a growl.

"Okay," said Jabari. "I think you'll be *s u r p r i s e d*… Wait right here, and I'll bring him to you."

Jabari made his way down the hill before disappearing around the corner. Z, Lefu, and Ellie looked at each other with questioning glances. A few minutes later, Jabari walked back with a short man following. The animals twitched and moved nervously, and Jabari attempted to calm them by placing Vicente behind himself.

With the sun beating down into the animal's eyes, and Vicente walking behind Jabari, it was only when Jabari stepped aside to introduce him, that the animals recognized him. "Vicente, these are my friends, Z, Ellie, O, and of course, you know

Lefu." Wide eyes formed on their faces, except for Lefu, who pulled his cheeks back exposing his fangs, his eyes hot with rage. The years of humiliation by The Sultan was inflamed by his anguish over home, and Vicente was presented like a lamb to the slaughter. Lefu lost all restraint. When Jabari finished speaking, he leaped into the air with a roar, headed straight for Vicente.

Jabari grabbed Vicente's arm and pulled him back and out of Lefu's path. But Lefu stretched out his right paw in mid-air and swiped at the left side of Vicente's head. The lion's momentum carried him past his target, and he landed on the grass beyond them. He dug his claws into the ground and scratched to a stop and turned to see blood trickling down Sultan's face and neck.

"Lefu, what are you doing! —We need him to get us home!"

Lefu was set on his prey, running on instinct fueled by rage —there was no turning back. With only a half-step forward, he leaped into the air again and protracted his claws—he could taste his victory.

"Lefu! Stop!" shouted Jabari.

Descending, Lefu's claws were upon Vicente's neck when they were suddenly yanked away as his body was slammed and thrown from his target. He hurled through the air with momentum, then tumbled and collapsed in the grass, breathless and still.

Vicente stood in a daze with blood stains on his shirt; bags of food lay where he dropped them.

The entire event took only a few seconds and left the group speechless, except for Ellie. She stood beside Vicente, her tusks raised high, angry and ready to knock Lefu to the ground again. "He might not want to go home, but I do!"

Jabari was about to respond, when he caught himself, realizing that talking to the animals in front of Vicente might not be the best thing to do—at least not yet. He turned his attention to Vicente who stood silent and motionless. Jabari took a handkerchief from his pocket and wiped the blood from Vicente's face as he assessed the damage. "You are very lucky Vicente… the cut is minor, you'll be fi…" His words trailed off as he saw blood running from a small puncture in Vicente's neck. "Did he get your neck, too?"

Vicente tried to respond, but only a raspy breath emerged. "Vicente, can you talk?"

❋ ❋ ❋

Lefu opened his eyes. His view appeared hazy at first, but soon cleared. He lay on his side in the grass, with shallow breaths and aching ribs. Though he knew where he was, he had no idea what happened or how long he'd been out. He rolled over in pain to get a view of the shelter and saw Ellie boring into him from behind her long tusks. He then understood that it was she who had swatted him like a fly into the air. He averted his eyes from her stare, wincing as he stood, then turned and trudged into the forest, every step an agony of disgrace. Ellie relaxed her protective stance over the group; she saw he wouldn't be any trouble…at least for the moment.

NINETEEN

Vicente sat on the floor of the shelter looking gaunt, pale and absent.

Jabari knelt beside him. "Vicente, you're in shock—let me help you." Vicente remained silent.

Jabari stretched out his arm. "Hand me your flask."

Vicente complied, head held low, staring at the ground.

"Lay down," said Jabari, firmly.

Vicente lowered himself. Anticipating a reaction, Jabari placed his left hand on Vicente's right shoulder and his right knee against Vicente's left arm. He then unscrewed the cap from the flask. He pushed Vicente's chin up and away from his body which opened a small puncture wound in his neck. Blood seeped out until Jabari poured a stream of alcohol from the flask into the wound. Vicente lay motionless with tears forming in his eyes, and when they could hold no more, they ran down the sides of his face. But it was only Vicente who understood that it wasn't pain that caused the tears, but joyful gratitude that he could feel the pain and the fear. Pain to remind him he was alive. Fear to remind him that he could lose what he'd considered throwing away before he met Jabari.

When the flask was empty, Jabari released his hold.

The ex-lion tamer turned his head toward Jabari and gurgled, "Thank you." For Vicente, the gratitude was for giving him purpose and meaning.

Jabari, thinking it was for helping him with his wounds,

replied, "You're welcome."

He then turned his attention to the animals and distributed the purchased food to Z, Ellie, and O. "I'm going to see Lefu," he announced and left the shelter carrying the bag of meat. He found the lion sitting high on the ridge, viewing the town. Jabari held out the food with a shaking arm. "I brought you some meat."

Lefu was famished, and he could smell it long before Jabari offered it to him. "Thanks…I won't hurt you." Jabari took the meat out of the bag and placed it in front of Lefu. The lion ripped and tore at it before swallowing a sizeable piece.

"Ellie said you have some issues about home," said Jabari.

Lefu looked at Jabari while chewing. "Not talkin' about it," came his terse, full-mouth response.

"Okay," Jabari replied. "You might have an issue, but the rest of us would like to go home. Is it so big that you won't travel with us?"

Lefu stopped tearing another piece of meat. His fear of being alone overshadowed his pain about home. "I guess I have a choice to make."

"Actually, you have two choices," said Jabari.

Lefu raised the skin over his right eye as Jabari continued. "First you have to get over your anger with Vicente since we can't get home without him." Lefu swallowed hard on another bite as Jabari walked away. Upon returning to the shelter, Jabari lay beside Vicente, took his knife from its pouch and handed it to him. "Here, take this."

The animals and Jabari drifted off to sleep as the light withdrew from the evening sky, but Vicente lay with his eyes open—his hand clenching the blade handle.

TWENTY

Vicente spent the night awake—terrified that every blowing leaf and forest noise was Lefu on the prowl. It wasn't until the comforting pre-dawn light arrived that he was relaxed enough to fall asleep. He rolled onto his back and let go of the knife, when Lefu stepped into the clearing, and a stillness settled over the forest. Prowling toward the logging shed, he kept his keen eyes focused on Vicente. He took short, hesitating steps, landing each paw intently. Closer and closer he moved, until he reached the edge of the shelter, only a short distance from his goal.

Vicente moved. Lefu froze and waited for him to become still again. *Only a few steps further,* he thought to himself. Now, only a hand length from Vicente's head, Lefu extended his neck —but instead of attacking him—he rubbed his cheek and mane across Vicente's face in a gesture of reconciliation.

Vicente jolted awake. Frightened in the fog of sleep, he clawed the ground for Jabari's knife.

Unaware of Vicente's intention, and despite the frantic movements below him, Lefu continued to nuzzle.

Vicente's fingers touched the edge of the handle. He grabbed a hold of the knife and pulled his arm back to drive it into Lefu, when Jabari's hand grabbed a hold of Vicente's wrist and held it back. "Vicente... it's ok!"

Jabari held it until Vincente realized what was happening.

He glanced at Jabari with wide eyes as Lefu continued to nuzzle him. The lion only stopped when Vincente's raspy, muffled laughter rose from under his shaggy mane. Vicente dropped the knife, turned over and lifted himself to his knees. He reached forward, placed his arms around Lefu's head, and hugged him with gratitude. He pulled himself back and beheld Lefu, no longer seeing an animal to fear, or a performer, but a regal creature in his own right.

TWENTY-ONE

Earlier that night.

Lefu also had a sleepless night wrestling with fears, but different than Vicente's. On the surface, he worried about the fate that might befall him without the protection of the group, but he was more frightened at the thought of being abandoned again. He hadn't had to face being alone since he was a cub, and now this torment was suffocating Lefu. He was no closer to overcoming it at first light, when leaves rustled high above in a tree. He looked up and saw O descending from the canopy until he settled on a low branch nearby. O handpicked a few leaves and chewed.

Lefu yawned. "What do you want?" he said, annoyed, though familiar with their routine as cage neighbors.

"Question what *you* want." said O in a level tone.

Lefu shot a look at O with dark, tired eyes.

O swallowed. "You no sleep?"

"Not a wink."

O continued to inspect the surrounding leaves. "You stubborn animal."

"Yeah, we've been over that before."

O chewed on a few choice leaves. "I tell you truth you no like."

"Maybe I'm more open than you think," said Lefu.

O stopped chewing. He reminded Lefu of their conversations when the defiant cub first joined the circus: "Small step, still a step."

Lefu nodded in familiar agreement. His old friend had changed little since he first met him and Lefu respected his strange companion, even though he didn't always understand him. "I realized something last night …" He lifted a paw and scratched his ear. "… even if I had killed Sultan, I wouldn't feel any better than I do now… Maybe for a while, but I'd still be the same… angry."

O received Lefu's revelation with pause. "…If kill Sultan no help, what anger about?"

Lefu studied the shadowy forest with an admission that took him many years to express. "I always thought I was strong and courageous… fearless." Lefu glanced up and met the orangutan's penetrating eyes. "…But I realize now that I'm just afraid." He then stared in resignation at the trees in front of him.

O let Z's words hang in the air before he spoke. "…Everyone afraid."

Lefu let out a long-held breath and rested his chin on his paws.

"When you face fear; you learn courage." said O.

Lefu's muscles tensed as he considered O's words, and while another long moment passed in quiet, his tension increased so much that his entire body trembled. "I don't… know how." Lefu exhaled in anguish.

O's eyes softened and he spoke as one does to a child. "That why it called courage… if you feel you can, you no need it."

Lefu looked up at O. He'd heard O's wisdom many times before, but this time Lefu's conflicted mind surrendered; his shaking ceased, and his stiff body relaxed. *I can do this* he thought to himself, then stood and made his way to the shelter.

TWENTY-TWO

Jabari, Vicente, and Lefu's laughter awakened Z and Ellie. Z stood and quivered his body to shake off his grogginess, when Ellie trumpeted at the sight of Lefu atop Vicente. Her horn put everyone on guard as they faced her.

"He's not angry!" blurted Jabari.

Ellie plowed dirt behind her foot, then lowered and raised her head while trumpeting.

Lefu nuzzled Vicente. "I'm not here to hurt anyone."

Ellie's tusks waved in the air like threatening swords.

Vicente placed one hand on Lefu and lifted the other in front of him toward Ellie to calm her. "It's ok," he rasped.

Ellie's snorted and her eyes darted between Vicente, Lefu, and Jabari. She made one more half push of dirt with her foot before letting out a "humph". Then her body relaxed, and she walked out from under the shelter.

"That was close." murmured Z with wide eyes.

❋ ❋ ❋

As the adrenaline from the conflict fell, other instincts rose. "Where are we going to get food for all of us?" asked Z.

Jabari turned to Vicente. "How much money do you have?"

"What for?" Vicente whispered with a rasp.

"For food; for us; for the animals."

Vicente nodded with an understanding look. To save his

injured vocal cords, he raised his left hand, and with his pointer and thumb, formed a zero.

Jabari's countenance fell. "There must be something we can do?" He then extended the message to his animal friends by catching their attention with his eyes.

Ellie returned to the edge of the shelter. "Why don't we do what we've always done?"

"What?" asked Z.

Ellie shuffled her feet. "We've been a circus for all these years, haven't we?" She rose her trunk like a question mark. "Why not continue for a little while longer… if it can get us home?"

Lefu shook his mane. "I spent my life hating the circus, and now we're free, and you want us to do it again!"

Vicente heard the animal sounds and wondered why they appeared bothered by one another. With Ellie trumpeting followed by Lefu growling, he feared another conflict and tried to calm them. "Lefu, it's okay." He rubbed the lion's mane while he looked at Ellie and said, "It's okay, Ellie; see we're friends."

Ellie rolled her eyes and continued her discussion. "I understand that Lefu, but what if we did it differently—our way?"

"What do you mean?" asked Lefu.

Z interjected with bright eyes and a beaming smile: "You mean like a petting zoo!" Lefu flicked his tail in agitation.

Ellie patted Z on his back with her trunk. "I don't know…I think maybe we can use what we know to our advantage."

"I'm not performing for anyone!" said Lefu, his fangs hanging just below his jowls.

"Me neither," said Z.

"Okay, so we agree that we don't want to perform, but people still want to experience us, right?" Ellie waited for an objection, but no one challenged her statement. "So why don't we give them at least that?" She looked from one to the other while the idea settled into their minds.

After a short period of silence, Lefu tried to articulate the concept as the words formed in him, "So… you want us… to stand there… and let people… look at us?"

The lion was about to laugh at his own words, when Jabari took over. "Vicente, why don't we start an animal touring group, with the proceeds going to return them home? No performances: just people experiencing these glorious animals without cages."

Vicente thought for a moment and nodded. "Yes," he gurgled.

"Yes!" said Jabari, then expanded Ellie's idea to Vicente. "No tricks; no cages; no whips; no performances; no leaders, and no owners."

As the momentum of Jabari's speech grew, the animals looked at one another for a sign of objection, but none came.

Jabari went on enthusiastically, "Just us together, letting people revere these creatures for who they are!" he concluded.

Z brayed with excitement and the elephant trumpeted, but Lefu remained silent.

"They really like your idea, Jabari," said Vicente with a chuckle.

There was a gleam in Jabari's eyes as he looked to his animal friends and smiled. "Yeah, it's like they really understand me."

TWENTY-THREE

Their first 'show' was only familiar to the group by name; aside from that, everything was different. No one knew how the show—if that's what they could even call it—would unfold. They had no real plan—just an idea strung together with excitement and hope, and some old materials salvaged by Vicente from the circus grounds the day prior. Jabari had scrawled flyers and distributed them in the nearby village:

> *Experience the majesty of incredible animals from afar—Up Close! Lion, Zebra, Elephant, and Orangutan. Experience them firsthand, without cages. Feel their presence and awe in their glory! All proceeds to fund their return home.*

On the morning of the show, Vicente and Jabari waited to greet people outside the improvised tent, which held Ellie, Lefu, Z and O. Vicente had tied a scarf around his neck to hide his wound, giving him an artistic flair. The first group to arrive at the grassy field at the edge of town was a family of four; A boy and girl giddy with excitement, with their parents who'd skeptically come at their children's insistence. The father cleared his throat. "You have *live* animals in that tent?"

Jabari stood confidently. "Yes."

The mother bit her lip. "With no *cages*?"

"They are very friendly and well trained." said Jabari.

The mother wrapped her arms around the boy and girl. "How can I be sure that my children will be safe?"

Vicente's enthusiasm overtook him. "I worked with the

THE END OF THE CIRCUS

lion myself for years—he's harmless!" but he strained his wound and winced. "Excuse me—" He whispered as he pointed to the handkerchief. "—I have a bit of a cold."

The callow boy tugged on his father's coat while looking up with eager eyes. "Please, please, Dad!" The man looked to his wife for approval, then nodded. "Okay then." He handed Vicente the small sum of money. Jabari stepped to the tent door, his eyes dancing in excitement at Vicente as he walked with the family in procession.

Overlapping flaps of canvas formed the tent door. When pulled back, it allowed the visitors to step into a gap, before a second canvas door. The two entries were so that onlookers couldn't see what was awaiting them inside as people came and went. The tent had no roof, and the white canvas was supported by poles made of branches, attached at the top to ropes that were pinned to the ground by crude wooden stakes outside. It wasn't much of a structure, but if the wind didn't kick up, and it didn't rain, it created the allure of mystery needed to entice the townspeople to pay the modest fare.

Jabari opened the makeshift tent door and walked the family inside: father, mother, daughter and eager son. Now inside the gap, he closed the exterior canvas drape and moved to the second flap. Jabari reached for it and was about lift it open, when he hesitated. Although he'd never been a part of a show, he'd seen enough of the Malcolm Brothers' performances to know that something more than opening the curtain was required. Jabari recalled an opening line and spoke in a deep voice not his own. "Ladies and gentlemen, welcome to..." Jabari's voice trailed off as he realized his performance wasn't becoming of their intention. Bewildered, the family looked at one another as Jabari gathered himself, but before they lost confidence, he re-captured their attention. He shifted his tone and whispered to them. "If you've been to a circus before, you would have heard things like how deadly, or how powerful, or how fierce these creatures are. Or perhaps you'd see animals trained to do things for your amusement." Jabari shook his head. "…That's not what this experience is about. You are going to meet firsthand, four very special animals. Animals that should not even be here, but by choosing to experience them, you will help return them home…where they belong."

Lefu, Ellie, Z, and O tuned their ears and listened to the kind words that came from Jabari.

"These animals were taken from their land, abused and used. They are weary and long for a better life, and you are now a part of their return."

Ellie struggled to hold back her tears as Jabari continued. "Before I open this canvas flap, I want you to each take food from the baskets in front of you."

The family made their way to them and the mother scooped a handful of the grains marked with a sign saying *Zebra*. Her daughter took a pear from the basket with the word *Orangutan* written on it. The father chose the meat marked *Lion*, and the boy took an apple from the basket labeled *Elephant.* When each of them had their food, Jabari pulled back the second canvas flap.

"Now, please walk slowly and quietly into the tent and stand in front of the animal that you have selected food for."

They stepped forward and their curiosity and excitement blended with reverence; no one spoke or moved as they stood before the animals—they were in awe. Jabari was going to direct them, when O reached out to the girl and gently took the pear from her hand. As his dark hand touched hers, she caught his gentle eyes and smiled, then glanced at her family, encouraging them. The father threw the small meat portion to Lefu, who gulped it down. Nervous, the man tittered, but stifled it when Lefu growled. *This is gonna be fun!* thought Lefu.

Z lipped the grains from the mother's cupped hands, producing a giggle, while the boy reached out toward Ellie, apple in hand.

Jabari let out a breath, pursed his lips, and looked up in relief.

TWENTY-FOUR

Ellie

The trainer yelled his command and hit the back of her front legs with a large bamboo stick, then drove the point of his bull hook into one of the sensitive spots on Ellie's head. She squealed in pain like a hurt child, and tossed her enormous head from side to side, refusing to obey the instruction to bend her knees. Again, the command came, and with it the point of the bull hook. Blood flowed from her pierced skin, but she remained resolute not to bend her knees.

She hated her trainer. She hated the circus. She hated her life. She hated the thought of performing, but most importantly, deep inside, she knew she could not give in.

Righteously rebellious, she knew what was wrong—the whole thing was wrong. *Who are they to tell me what to do! Why do I have to perform tricks, but not them? Who gave them the right to control me!*

The pain of the third blow was staggering, but she refused to comply. She was weak from her lack of food—her trainer's way of making her more compliant—tired from lack of sleep, bloodied and bruised. She knew too well how this would end, as this had become her daily routine. She'd be forced back to her trailer, shackled with insufficient water, only to begin again, early the following day.

The fourth blow was beyond her ability to stand. Pain shot through her entire body and she dropped to her knees, unwittingly drawing praise from the trainer, which she resented. Anger burned within her. She knew she could reach up with her trunk, throw him off her back and crush him underfoot, but she knew that would also be *her* end. While she considered it, her trainer lowered himself to the side of her head, holding the rope fastened around her neck. He pushed three large apples into her gaping mouth, then patted her and spoke more words of praise. In her weakness, Ellie chewed and swallowed the apples. The sugar flooded into her blood and gave her energy she'd long been missing. She didn't make a choice, so much as the inevitable occurred; she couldn't kill him, and she couldn't keep resisting. Ellie accepted her fate and bent her knee. She no longer hated her life, her trainer, or the circus, but instead began to quietly hate herself.

TWENTY-FIVE

With a nervous smile, the boy looked to his father for assurance as he handed the elephant the apple, but his father's eyes went wide as Ellie thrust herself up onto her hind legs. Unsure of what was happening, everyone looked in surprise, but as she reached the top of her ascent, she let out a loud, angry trumpet, putting everyone on notice. As she descended, her ears folded open, enlarging her head, and her front legs kicked in mid-air protest. Ellie swayed with every bend of her knees, and her tusks swung from side to side as though an invisible swarm of insects attacked her. Jabari grabbed the hand of the boy and yanked him toward himself and the other family members.

"Ellie, it's okay," said Jabari in a calming tone. He approached her with his arm extended, but she thrust herself away and rose on her hind legs again. Fearful of the family being trampled, Jabari pushed them toward the back of the tent. Ellie stampeded out. The tent ropes over the door caught on her forehead and ripped the pegs from the ground and the canvas flowed after her. The family ducked and the exposed and frightened animals darted in all directions as onlookers shrieked and ran.

The now-embarrassed and frightened woman gathered her children in her arms and screamed at Jabari: "Safe! You call this safe! We could have been killed!" Her son sobbed. She gathered him in her arms and squeezed him tight to her chest. "You should be arrested for this. What was I thinking, getting into this tent with these animals?" Jabari held his head low and knew better than to speak too soon. He remained silent as the woman cursed him until she exhausted her anger. When she had no more words, Jabari said, "I'm sorry." He waited again in the silence that followed, and when he sensed it was safe, he continued: "I don't know why she became so agitated. I think she was frightened somehow. She meant no harm; I'm sure." The family departed and the mother continued to condemn the events to her husband as they walked away.

Jabari and Vicente joined the animals who had gathered inside the forest edge at the far side of the field. Together, they followed the path of toppled small trees until they caught up with Ellie, standing atop a knoll, looking over the village from inside the edge of dense forest. She knew her friends were there, but she ignored them.

Jabari stepped toward her head from behind her right side. "Ellie, are you okay?"

She remained silent and didn't move.

Jabari continued to advance slowly, and when he stood close enough to see her eyes, he saw she was crying and no longer angry. He raised his hand cautiously toward her neck, and when she offered no resistance, he rested his hand against her front leg. Now sure of acceptance, he moved in, leaned closer, and held her with his arms spread wide—as best one can hold a sobbing elephant.

Ellie reached around with her trunk and wrapped it around Jabari. Z, O, and Vicente stood and watched, giving her space.

After a few minutes, Ellie sniffled. "I'm sorry everyone… I didn't mean to ruin everythi…" She sobbed.

Z took a few steps forward and leaned against her side to comfort her. "It's okay, Ellie… sometimes you can't control when it comes out."

Her sobbing ceased for a moment and a sniffle came from her trunk. "Damn apples."

Vicente and O followed Z's lead, and came in close and

held themselves against her, while Lefu looked on from a distance.

Ellie let out an enormous trumpet sigh of relief and laughed. The others joined in, and the energy of the group shifted from consolation to resolution.

❉ ❉ ❉

Fearful of repercussions from Ellie's breakdown, they returned to the field and gathered up the tent and their supplies, loading everything on Ellie and Z. O rode atop Ellie at the end of the procession on the dirt road. With branches tied to her tail to cover their tracks, they headed south toward Port City. Jabari had spent what little money he had left on the flyers and the food for the show. They didn't know what lay ahead, only where they couldn't stay, and the direction they needed to go.

TWENTY-SIX

Discouragement lay heavy on the group and they walked without speaking for some time, before stopping to rest at a pond they spotted from the roadside. They tucked themselves behind bushes and trees growing between the road and pond. The animals drank and refreshed themselves with the cool water, resting afterwards on the soft, lush grass at the water's edge.

Vicente and Jabari sat on the grass and watched their animal friends with concern. Jabari took a pensive sip from his canteen and caught Vicente's eye. "There's something I need to tell you."

Vicente unscrewed the cap from his canteen. "…Go on."

Jabari took another sip and swallowed hard. "I didn't tell you before…in part because I wasn't sure I knew how, and I also wasn't sure… if I could trust you."

Vicente frowned, took a drink and closed his canteen. "Ah huh."

Jabari rubbed the back of his neck. "If we're in this together… you need to know something…I don't quite know how to tell you this, but… um…."

"Get on with it!" Vicente rasped.

Jabari stared at Vicente. "…I can talk with the animals."

For a moment, Vicente remained silent, holding Jabari's gaze. Then what began as a slight curve of his lips lifting his thin mustache, shifted to a broad smile. He looked at Jabari and his eyes widened, and his entire expression grew more expansive.

He chuckled, at first trying to control himself and then, looking away and at the animals, he laughed, then winced in pain. "Good one, Jabari," he chuckled.

Jabari crossed his arms. "Are you done?"

Vicente's face transformed from laughter to disbelief. "You're serious? You really think you can talk to the animals?... I thought you were joking!" He looked at young Jabari and burst into laughter so hard that he rolled onto his side and curled up, only to lift his torso, look again, then roll back onto the ground howling. With every outburst, he recoiled in pain, paused for relief, then burst into another round of anguished laughter.

Jabari waited until the laughter subsided. "Are you done now?"

Vicente gaped at Jabari with wet eyes and tears on his cheeks. Jabari stood firm; his jaw clenched.

Feeling sorry for Jabari, Vicente wiped his face and gathered himself. "Amigo, I have worked with animals for years, and I can tell you that isn't possible."

"I didn't think so either."

The animals looked on at the exchange with intrigue.

Vicente raised his eyebrows and donned a patronizing tone. "Okay... what makes you think you can talk with the animals?"

"I just can; I can't explain how."

"All right then, why don't you show me?" said Vicente, now with a hint of condescension.

Jabari put a hand to his chin. "All right... let me see... how could I show you?"

Vicente suggested in a mocking tone. "Ask something that only Lefu would know about me."

"Great idea!" Jabari turned to the lion. "Lefu, what can you tell me about Vicente that would prove that we can talk with each other?"

Vicente tilted his head and sighed in pity.

Lefu made a few growls and Jabari turned to Vincente. "Lefu said he gave you a scar on your back soon after you took over the show."

Vicente's eyes went wide for a moment before he drew his eyebrows together and tilted his head. "A lot of people know that Jabari. You could have heard that from the circus. You'll have to do a lot better than that if you expect me to believe you."

Frustrated, Lefu roared. "Ask him if the name Louisa means anything."

Jabari nodded and addressed Vicente. "Who's Louisa?"

Fear appeared in Vicente's eyes and his cheeks flushed. "Who?" he asked with feigned innocence.

"He's lying," growled Lefu.

"Um-hum," breathed Jabari as though not speaking to Lefu at all.

Vicente's brow furrowed. "I don't know anyone named Louisa."

Jabari rubbed his forehead and tried to spare Vicente embarrassment. "Maybe I misunderstood him. Lefu, can you tell me something *else* that you know about Vicente?"

"I know he's *lying*" Lefu rumbled back.

"Something *else* perhaps?" Jabari continued as though Lefu had not spoken.

Lefu roared in frustration at both Vicente and Jabari. "Tell him that Louisa is his daughter!"

Jabari was conflicted; He needed Vicente, and he didn't want to lose him over something he clearly didn't want known. With nothing else offered by Lefu, he stammered: "…Lefu said… Louisa… is your daughter."

TWENTY-SEVEN

Vicente

"No more bets," said the croupier as the roulette wheel turned.

Vicente stood at the crowded casino table in the early hours of the morning, with an intensity not shared by the other gamblers. He was gaunt, pale and sweaty, with a nervousness that made him stand apart from the laughter and excitement around him. He'd been at the table for many hours, and although he was drained, he couldn't leave.

As the ball whirled around the wheel, Vicente retreated to the silence of his mind. He tried to block out what the ball's destiny held for him if it was not favorable. Though he'd wagered many times, and, in many ways, this bet was different. It was no longer about winning; it was about not losing—this gamble was for his life.

"No more bets," repeated the croupier.

It didn't matter to Vicente, as everything he had, rested on the black felt. He lifted his drink from the table to take a sip and pitied the murky, twisted portrait reflected at him from the ice in his glass.

Experience told him when the orb would fall. Attuned to the game, he knew the moment it would drop from the upper ridge of the wheel and he lifted his eyes from his glass to watch it bounce off the first number.

He'd gambled away everything he had, and even much that he didn't; squeezing everything he could from family and friends. Now, what he had left on the altar, including his life, awaited judgment.

The ball bounced high off the first number and careened to the opposite side, bouncing yet again to another section of the wheel as it spun. Other gamblers shouted their numbers in the hope of a win, but the excitement that he used to feel at this moment had left him long ago, although part of him continued to hope that it would return.

He stood in a trance and watched the ball move as though in slow motion, bouncing erratically on the rotating wheel. His face remained blank as he followed the marble to its ultimate destiny—as though he already knew the outcome.

"Red, 16," exclaimed the croupier, exciting a young, fashionable couple opposite him.

Vicente threw back the last of his drink, set his glass down, and stepped away from the table. He walked out of the casino and left town without ever looking back, leaving everything and everyone he knew and loved—including his two-year-old daughter, Louisa.

TWENTY-EIGHT

The only thing stronger than Vincente's love for Louisa was his own shame. To think of Louisa was to think about his failed life, the debts to family that he walked away from, and the money he lost. Her memory was precious, but painful; a constant reminder of what he saw as his failed existence. Having Jabari know this was a painful affront to his fragile self-image. He was ill prepared to face exposure, as well as the realization that Jabari could speak with the animals. "I'm gonna take a walk," he said as he stood and sauntered away, downcast.

"Well, I guess we proved it," said Lefu.

Jabari shot him a look. "You couldn't have picked something smaller?"

Lefu swung his tail in satisfaction. "I forgave him, but he needed a reality check."

"What is that supposed to mean?"

Lefu shook his main at Jabari. "Taking off the Sultan suit and helping us is great, but if we're going to trust him, isn't he going to have to trust us too?"

Jabari's lips pursed. "I thought about that when you said it, I just didn't think this was the best time."

O paused from grooming the long hair on his arms. "Truth not usually invited… it show up to see how we say hello. We know soon if he trust and be trust."

The animals nodded their agreement as the setting sun warmed and comforted them while they rested in the soft grasses. Reminded of home, Ellie shifted the conversation. "Do you think it will be the same when we get home again."

"I hope so," said Z, picturing in his mind, herds of his kind on the grassy Savannah.

"I'm scared and excited," said Ellie, looking at O for comfort.

O's eyes softened but his speech was strong. "Ellie, you are strongest animal of all. You should no fear."

"Me? Strong?" said Ellie with a disbelieving yet flattered look on her face. She curled her trunk. "I'm not strong."

O stood up tall with certainty in his eyes. "You are *strongest* one. You have pain, but you keep heart open—this big love—take highest strength and courage! ...most become pain when they get pain." Lefu and Z hunched and looked at the ground as he continued. "Very strong to no stop love."

"But I gave up my fight. I'm *not* strong," Ellie protested.

"You still no see..." O gazed into her moist eyes. "...You give up what you must—the outside—but you no give up inside... You beautiful and strong... You *always* be."

Ellie's tears flowed at O's words, and she lifted her trunk to dry her eyes. She'd never seen herself through eyes of love and never gave thought to anything more than what she saw as her failure. "Thank you, O, that means more to me than you can know."

"You welcome..." O scratched his back. "...You no pain to others, but you pain to you."

Ellie looked into O's eyes; they were as rich and loving as his words.

"Only love you no give is to you... time you love Ellie again."

Ellie gasped as something deep and profound stirred within. Her thinking ceased as pieces of her emotional puzzle flipped in her stomach—pieces she had battled with for years—surrendered and joined together.

O sauntered away from the group as Jabari excused himself. "I'm going to see if I can find Vicente." He stood and made his way to the road, continuing in the direction in which he'd seen Vicente walk.

The dirt road soon came to a high spot, giving him a long view of it, and the grassy fields on either side. In the distance he saw Vicente, sitting—for the second time—under a large tree, facing the road, leaning against its trunk, head down. Jabari made his way there, squatted and leaned next to him. He waited a few minutes to give Vicente a chance to speak, and when nothing came, he asked, "How old is she?"

Without looking up, Vicente reached into his pocket and carefully unfolded, and then opened, a well-worn envelope. He extracted from it a small picture of himself, holding a smiling toddler at his chest. He handed Jabari the treasured photograph like the work of art that it was.

Jabari grasped the edges in the same way it was handed to him, and he smiled at the happiness in their faces. "She's beautiful." he said, as he studied them in the black-and-white photo. The toddler had dark, curly hair to her shoulders, and she was smiling from ear to ear, almost laughing, with a delighted sparkle in her dark, wide eyes.

Vicente gave a sad eyed smile. "She's 9 now."

"You looked happy." Jabari passed the picture back to Vicente.

"I was." Vincente took the picture, studied it again, then reverently returned it to the envelope and folded it back into its former shape. "Whenever I think of her, I pull out this picture, and tell her I love her." Vicente put the envelope back in his pocket.

Jabari sensed both the love and the pain as Vicente spoke, and he couldn't help but note the contrast between the risk-taking lion tamer and the wounded, loving man. He couldn't hold the question that burned within him any longer. "Why aren't you with her?" he asked softly with respect for Vicente's vulnerability.

Vicente shuffled his feet. "It's a long story."

Jabari gave a relaxed smile. "Time, we have."

"Let's just say that I can't go back again."

Jabari waited again, hoping more was forthcoming, but without a response, he asked his other burning question: "Why did you lie to me about not having any family when you joined the circus?"

Vicente affixed his eyes on his feet again. "It's not something I'm proud of."

Jabari nodded. "I understand." He decided to not push things further—at least not for now. Instead, he reached into his satchel and reciprocated Vicente's offering and put forward a family photo of his father and mother, with young Jabari atop his mother's knee "This is my family."

Vicente received it with a smile, sharing the kinship of loneliness.

"My father died when I was five," Jabari explained, "and I have not seen my mother in almost a year." Vicente returned the picture. Forlorn, Jabari slipped it back into his satchel and he looked at Vicente. "Perhaps when this is all over, we'll both be home with those we love."

Vicente grimaced then raised his eyebrows hopefully. "I've been thinking about something else I think you might want to hear."

"Go on," said Jabari, intrigued.

Vicente pointed to the only home in view. "You see that house across the road up on the hill?"

"Yeah, what about it?"

TWENTY-NINE

The wooden farmhouse was similar to many others they'd seen while traveling with the circus, except it was very weather worn—so much so that sections of the faded white paint and green trim had altogether disappeared. It sat atop a hill, facing the road, with the peak of a black barn roof visible behind it. The grass was over-grown, even on the path to the door, and the roof of the house showed signs of needing repair.

"A place out of harm's way..." said Vicente, "... where they need us, and we need them."

Jabari knit his brow together. "What do you have in mind?"

Vicente got up and extended his hand to lift Jabari. "Follow me."

They walked the path to the house that led to a small, wooden doorstep resting on bricks. Torn mesh dangled from the side of the old screen door that squeaked when Vincente opened it. He rapped three times on the wooden door behind it. With barely enough room for both on the doorstep, they stood with their heads turned sideways, listening, but heard nothing. Vicente knocked again, this time, much harder, using his fist.

"Geez!" Jabari jumped in surprise, then collected himself.

Vicente gave a wry smile.

"Hold on, hold on," came the muffled words from the house. "Hold your horses," a gruff woman's voice echoed, followed by "I'm coming." a few seconds later.

The door swung open, revealing a stern looking woman, late in years with skin that had seen too many days in the sun. The visitors looked down, seeing why there were no footsteps heard; she sat in a wheelchair, her hands resting on the armrests. Her brown and gray hair fell on the shoulders of a white house coat, that was clean and bright in contrast to the dull house. "Hello…" she said, eyeballing the thin mustached man and the dark-skinned boy, both of whom backed up off the doorstep, and onto the grass. "…What can I do for you?"

Unsure, Jabari looked to Vicente who was still holding the screen door open with his left hand. "My friend and I need food and shelter. We have nowhere to go and we noticed your farm … we thought—" He looked around the house in a non-judgmental way. "—maybe you could use some help?"

The woman gave no sign of interest.

Jabari came forward a half step and raised his hand to interject. "We could give your house a bright coat of paint—" He smiled and glanced at her housecoat. "—bright and white like your robe!"

A twinkle flashed in her eyes as she put a finger to her chin and pressed her lips together.

"We can sleep in the barn." said Vicente, as a black cat appeared at the door and wound its way around the old woman's legs, one of which was wrapped in a cast to her knee.

"Where you boys from?" she asked.

"We used to work with the circus that burned down," Vicente replied.

The old woman bent herself forward, inviting the cat to her lap. It pounced into her arms and rested itself against her chest. She petted it with long, full body strokes. "I heard about that … those poor animals."

Jabari stared at his hands. "We lost many of our friends."

Vicente attempted to get the conversation back on track. "We worked with animals and we could help with yours."

"Other than this one, I don't have any—" The cats tail flipped in satisfaction. "—not since my husband passed." She focused on the now-purring cat, reminiscing over what she'd lost. Feeling sorry for them, and hopeful for the possibility of company, she continued without looking up. "I'll tell you what… let's see how you do tomorrow…you can stay in the barn tonight."

Vicente glanced a smile at Jabari and then extended his hand to the old woman. She looked up, and he rasped his name, "Vicente."

"Mabel," she returned with a firm handshake.

The younger extended his hand in kind with a bright smile. "Jabari."

"Nice to meet you Jabari," she said as they shook hands.

"You too."

"I've been wanting to get this place painted for years…" She looked up to reference what only they could see from the outside. "…It'll be good to get this place looking new again."

Jabari and Vicente looked at the paint together, and Jabari piped in with youthful optimism, "We'll have it looking good as new!"

They smiled for a moment, then Vicente brought closure: "We have a few things down the road by the pond. We'll collect them and return in a bit… do you mind if we take a quick look in the barn first?"

"Go right ahead. Just knock when you're back so I know you're here, but you'll have to get yourselves settled." She tapped the cast on her right leg. "As you can see, I'm a little house bound right now."

"Yes, ma'am," Vicente rasped.

Jabari and Vicente turned and walked away, excited for what they'd accomplished, and when they were far out of earshot, Jabari spoke. "What about the animals? We didn't tell her about them."

Vicente looked at Jabari. "Do you think she would have said yes if we'd told her?"

Jabari sighed. "I suppose not."

As they walked to the barn, Jabari expressed his concerns.

"But what are we going to do with them?"

Vicente opened the barn door and looked in. "They're coming with us."

Jabari poked his head inside. "What if she finds out?"

"So? What's the risk? We wind up exactly where we are now."

Jabari furrowed his brow, "I suppose."

Vicente closed the barn door. "What are you afraid of?"

"I don't know," said Jabari.

Vicente placed his hand on Jabari's shoulder. "Something I learned when I was training with the lions…if you're gonna do great things, you can't give way to fear."

Jabari forced a smile, confused by Vicente's contradiction as it related to Louisa.

Vicente put his hand on the back of Jabari's neck and affectionately shook him from side to side, then rubbed his curls. A warm feeling flowed through Jabari; despite its people, distractions, and excitement, the circus had been a lonely place for Jabari, and it had been a long time since he'd felt a kinship with another human being.

❊ ❊ ❊

The animals were waiting at the pond behind the cover of trees and bushes for Jabari and Vicente to return. As the two approached, the animals could see that their attitudes had shifted. Gone were the faces of concern, replaced with smiles and excitement.

"We have shelter for tonight." Vicente told the animals. "And if we do things right, maybe for a while!" When Vicente discerned from their sounds and movements that they'd understood his announcement, he explained about the widow and the farm. Jabari watched, incredulous, as Vicente talked to the animals as though he'd been doing it his entire life. He didn't understand *them*, as they asked him many questions, none of which he answered. When Vicente had finished, Jabari filled in the blanks. "We saw some food—there are fruit trees and some feed bags still in the barn. We have to figure out how to feed you, Lefu, but we can probably do some hunting and get something for you along the way. We'll have a roof over our heads, out of harm's way, with food and water—we couldn't ask for more." Jabari concluded to the quiet acceptance of the group.

After waiting until it was dark, they made their way along the road and stopped behind trees across from the old farm.

"Wait here until you see us enter the barn, but make sure no one is coming on the road" said Vicente to the animals before he and Jabari walked to the house.

Vicente gave two quick knocks, then a third then he and Jabari waited in the light over the step until Mabel appeared.

Vicente held up his canteen as justification for their departure. "We're ready to settle in for the night."

"Okay, boys; here's a lantern for you," passing it to Jabari. "Let me know if you need anything."

"Thanks!" said Jabari.

They traipsed around the side of the house and headed toward the barn. Jabari walked with the lamp hung low on his arm with Vicente between him and the house. The lamp projected their shadows high on the wall, reminding Jabari of the fateful night at the circus. He hoped it wasn't a bad omen.

Once at the barn, they slipped inside, closed the door and looked around. Ample bales of hay were stacked in the loft, and the large barn had plenty of room for everyone to sleep. They'd only been there a minute or so when Ellie swung the door open with her trunk. The lantern on the floor in the middle of the barn cast a bright light out the open door. Vicente suspected silhouettes of the four arrivals were visible from several windows in the house. He dove in front of the lantern to block its light, then wrenched the dimmer to low. "Get in, quickly!" The animals charged into the barn in darkness.

Jabari pulled the door shut and rested his forehead against it. "I hope she didn't see that."

Vicente turned up the lantern, exhaled and shot Jabari a

look of concern. "Si."

THIRTY

The first day on the farm confirmed Jabari's intuition. Mabel directed them to where they could find everything they needed to get started on the painting. Scrapers, paint, brushes, all sat ready in the shed, remnants of her former husband's unfinished plans. They began by scraping off the old, flaked paint to prepare the surface. Vicente had painted before, and he provided guidance to Jabari. "It does no good to paint without first taking off the old, otherwise the new won't stick."

Mabel smiled as she listened from the nearest window. Pleased with Vicente's confidence and skill, and Jabari's friendly attitude and hard work, by the end of the day, she'd decided that she liked them, and allowed them to stay. She explained that they could tend to and eat from the garden, have access to the fruit trees, and even hunt on her land, which was welcome news for Lefu.

Lonely for company, Mabel made fast friends with Jabari and Vicente over the dinners she prepared that first week. But she found it such good fun listening to their stories, and sharing her life with them, that it soon turned into two meals a day, then all three. As difficult as it was to prepare food in her condition, she felt joy in giving and being appreciated. To hear and see the gratitude when they came with excitement for each meal, gave her a sense of purpose that she hadn't had in a long time.

Besides food and shelter, the animals gained some semblance of freedom; the side door of the barn was hidden from view from the house windows and they calculated that if Ellie walked the right path from *that* door to the woods, even she couldn't be seen. It gave them safe passage to many acres of sanctuary, and each morning, Jabari, Vicente, Ellie, or O, lifted the latch to open the side door for the animals to forage and feed. They then made their way to their favorite pond, stream, field, or forest, and each evening at dusk, they returned to the sanctuary of the barn. It wasn't long before their freedom had its effect.

"Do you feel like everything is brighter and more vibrant," Z asked one afternoon while grazing near Ellie.

"I thought it was just me," she replied with a surprised, yet knowing look on her face.

Z paused chomping. "It's like I never noticed anything around me before… like I was just going through the motions." He took a moment to look at Ellie to be sure she understood.

She was wide eyed and gave a quick, up and down shake of her trunk. "I get it!"

Z stared across the fields. "Ever since I let go of the fear inside, I haven't been the same. I see things differently now. Everything—you, me… *life*. It used to be me against the world, and now… I feel a part of everything."

Ellie's eyes shone and she half smiled at him. "Plus, you're not a jerk anymore." Z caught her eye and a broad, gummy smile spread across his face.

As the days turned into weeks, Ellie and Z recovered from the many years of imposed identity. Gone were the cages and confinement, rulers and ringmasters. Gone were the schedules, and expectations, and what had been dormant awakened in them. No longer were they the object of someone else's purpose. At first this made them insecure—not having a role left them anxious. But with no immediate threat, nowhere to go, and needing no one's approval or disapproval, their anxiety faded. They resonated with their true identity, as the sentient and free beings they were. They now knew that they were much more than what they did for others, and that awareness brought them a peace they'd never experienced.

❈ ❈ ❈

Z shivered in the crisp fall air after taking a drink from a babbling brook, when Ellie challenged the group, "What are we doing here?"

Lefu tilted his head. "I thought we agreed we liked this spot."

"Not *here,* the stream, I mean *here,* the farm."

"Oh," said Z, acknowledging that he too was confused.

Ellie raised the skin over her eyes. "I thought we were supposed to be going *home*?"

Lefu licked his lips. "I like it here."

"We all like it better than the circus—" Ellie's voice had a 'that's-obvious' tone to it. "—This place has been great, and I'm not the same as when we came here… but I want more." A well of emotion pushed up in her, causing tears to form in her eyes. "I don't want to hide anymore… I want to be free. Free to roam. Free to trumpet as loudly as I want. Free to run anywhere. Free to be me. Free to be." Tears rolled down her face. "All this sneaking is like I'm still caged." The group remained silent in the face of her palpable anguish until Lefu stood. "We should be thankful we're here."

Z looked at the trees that were changing their color. "Ellie's right; besides, we can't stay here forever; winter's coming." He then turned to O, who sat on the grass at the edge of the stream watching it flow. "What do you think?"

A moment passed before he responded. "Truth in your heart…you feel it when Ellie speak… Always follow heart." He turned his head back to the flowing water. "Then like stream… you flow to destiny."

Ellie stretched her trunk and touched O's shoulder. "How did you get so wise?"

Z brayed: "Yeah, we all know each other's stories, but we

know nothing about your life."

O eyed them before responding. "Like you…" He pointed to his audience. "…I take from home very young." He cupped his hands close together to show how small he'd been. "Human try make me be like people. I not good human…" He turned and lifted the hair on his back to expose multiple scars. "…They whip me."

Lefu and Z flushed and their eyes went wide.

Ellie winced, understanding the pain. "I am so sorry."

"Thank you, but no sorry—More story. Many year in small cage alone. Long time, very sad. Old Thai monk buy me and take me home. He have same gift as you, Jabari. He teach me most special truth … love and accept." O put his hands over his heart, and his eyes softened. "Then, I see…" He pinched the skin on his arm for emphasis. "…I not orangutan you see." He pointed to his head, "I not brain either. I learn who I am. I find *secret* me." He pointed to his stomach. "Magic me, deep inside —then no more suffer." A peaceful smile blossomed on his face, and he paused, reminiscing, before his countenance saddened. "Then monk pass on. I go circus. Very sad again for long time. Then remember true me again. Still in cage, but no more sad. Then go to Malcolm Circus."

Z mouth hung open, shaken. "That's terrible!"

"No terrible. I have special job."

Ellie, Z, and Lefu glanced at one another, unable to comprehend his optimism and sense of purpose.

Ellie scrunched her face. "What special job?"

"Help animal in circus no suffer. To no be lonely." He pointed again to his stomach. "To help them find magic inside."

"That explains a lot," said Z, remembering his own encounter with O.

Ellie nodded in agreement. "You do it well, O. I've been trying to love myself for years, but somehow, what you said touched me more than anything before."

O turned his kind eyes to his friends, curled his long fingers, and pointed to his stomach. "Words from magic place, *most* powerful. Can change *whole* world."

❋ ❋ ❋

When the animals returned to the barn that evening, they listened to updates from Jabari and Vicente about Mabel, the chores they performed, and any news that Mabel shared over their meals. But that evening, as Vicente talked about the activities of the day, Ellie interrupted with a soft, but clear trumpet.

"What?" said Jabari.

"What?" Vicente asked, not realizing that Ellie had spoken.

"We want to go home," Ellie said.

Vicente realized that Ellie and Jabari were conversing, "What did she say?"

Jabari tilted his head and raised his eyebrows. "She said they want to go home."

"What? Why? We have everything we need here: food, shelter, privacy. What more could we want?"

"We want to go *home*," Ellie repeated then stared at Jabari and Vicente, "We really appreciate all that you two have done for us. We don't know what would have become of us and we are eternally thankful for your kindness." She paused long enough to let Jabari relay the words to Vicente, before she continued. "Do you know what it's like to not be free? Do you know what it's like to be looking over your shoulder all day, afraid that you'll be found out? Being in the circus was awful, but being out of the circus, and being afraid is just another cage… only with bars you can't see."

Jabari echoed her words again. Emotion choked Vicente. He looked at Jabari, and then at the faces of each animal, beginning with Ellie, and ending with O, who sat above them in the rafters. He understood Ellie as he was reminded of his own fear: fear of failure; fear of being discovered; fear of shame. More so, he sensed something when he looked at them. Something familiar told him she was right. He realized that what he saw in them, was what he saw when he looked at Louisa's picture; something he was previously unwilling to accept. It was an urging for more than what he imposed upon them in his mind; the idea that they were safe and taken care of, and that should be enough; that they were better off the way things were. He knew in his heart what their hearts were saying, and he surrendered to Ellie and what Louisa's picture had been saying to him all along—that he, like them, belonged home.

Vicente's brow furrowed and his lips pursed.

"What's the matter?" asked Jabari.

"…I don't know how I'm gonna to do this," he mumbled in a daze, speaking to himself. "I don't know how I'm going… to face them."

Jabari then understood that Vicente wasn't thinking of the animals, but of Louisa and his family.

Vicente paced. Shame, the weight of his debts, and fear of rejection by his family and friends, overtook him. Dread seized his mind as he realized that everything he had avoided, collided in this singular decision. Sweat ran down his face as his pacing became more agitated—back and forth in the barn he marched, mumbling. He turned once again to pace back from where he came, but halted abruptly, blocked by O's inverted head. O hung upside down, suspended from the rafters and gazed into Vicente's fear-filled eyes.

O sensed Vicente's conflict and fear, and he stretched out his enormous hands and enveloped Vicente's entire head. O made a few of his familiar sounds while continuing to hold Vicente's gaze.

Vicente kept his eyes fixed on O, "…What did he say?" he asked Jabari.

Jabari translated in full English. "The universe always supports the highest intentions of the heart."

O's hands and words penetrated and dissipated Vicente's fear, and as the haze left him, Vicente's expression returned to its former state. He composed himself, patted his hands on his sweat-soaked shirt, said a quiet thank you to O, and walked out of the barn.

Astonished by what happened, Jabari followed to check on Vicente. "Are you okay?" he asked as he caught up to him.

Vicente stopped and looked at his younger friend with hesitation, thinking he wouldn't understand what he had to face. He dropped his head and let out a heavy breath, releasing the pressure.

Jabari formed a half smile. "A good man once told me that if you're gonna do great things, you can't give way to fear."

A long moment of silence fell between them. Jabari's face appeared both concerned and hopeful. He had tested the relationship and wasn't sure if it would survive.

Vicente lifted his head and gazed at Jabari. "When we first met on the logging road…" Vicente hesitated as he formed his words, "…I never told you why I wanted to help you."

"You told me it would mean a lot to you." said Jabari.

Vicente continued in a heavy voice, "That 'meaning a lot' meant more than you could know." Jabari scrunched his face.

Vicente looked at the ground before looking back up at Jabari. "I was thinking of ways to end it all."

Jabari's eyes went wide for a moment before his face softened with compassion. "I… had no idea." Vicente remained silent, which gave Jabari time to think of something encouraging to say. "Then you were intended for better things… even if they are hard."

Vicente smiled at Jabari and tucked his shirt into his pants. "I guess it's time to play cards." He threw his hair back with his hands, raised his eyebrows and exhaled. "This will be the biggest gamble of my life." He then turned and walked away.

THIRTY-ONE

The following morning, after enjoying a breakfast of Mabel's frequent oatmeal, Vicente took charge, "Let me get the dishes today, Mabel—it's the least I can do." He then addressed Jabari. "I'll catch up soon."

Though uneasy, Jabari left the house to begin the chores they'd planned the prior evening.

Vicente began to clear the table. "Mabel, you've been so good to us over the past months."

Mabel moved to the counter aided by crutches. "You boys are wonderful, and you know I love having you here."

"I do, and … hem … that's what makes telling you this so hard."

Mabel stopped, a blank look on her face.

Vicente stopped clearing. "We have to leave."

"What do you mean, you have to leave?" Mabel's countenance fell.

Vicente put his hand on his chin. "We have to take care of some things, so we have to go."

"Is there anything I can do to help? Do you have to leave to get them done?"

He picked up a few more dishes from the table. "Yes, we have to go, and I don't think you can help."

"I'm sorry to hear that." she said, staring at the empty plates. "I'm really going to miss you two."

"And us you," Vicente said as their eyes connected. He

stepped forward and gave her a warm hug. "Thank you for all you have done for us. You can't imagine how much you've helped us all." Vicente blinked rapidly, realizing what he'd said.

Mabel turned back to the counter. "So…how do you plan to take the animals with you?"

Vicente's body tensed, and his mind raced. He rested the dishes on the counter. *Had they been careless? Had she heard Ellie or Lefu?*

Mabel turned to face him. "I knew since the night you arrived."

Vicente recalled the lantern on their first night. "You've known all this time? Why… Why didn't you say anything?"

"I've been so lonely since I lost my husband and I was desperate for friendship. When I realized how good it was to have you around, I wasn't going to risk that. Besides, this way I could deny it if anyone else found out."

Vicente raised an eyebrow. "Anyone else?"

Mabel lowered her head and raised her eyebrows. "There's a reward for them."

Vicente leaned back. "A reward? … We didn't steal them."

Mabel held her gaze and Vicente squirmed. He nodded his head side to side, then surrendered the story; he told her how the Malcolm Brothers had burned down the circus, how Jabari had saved the animals, how they'd met, and their failed effort to raise money to get them to Port City for the long voyage home.

Mabel's eyes went wide. "Wow!"

Vicente tensed, unable to interpret her response.

Mabel eyed him up. "Don't worry…I believe you."

Vicente's body relaxed.

She turned and hobbled to a sideboard that sat against the far wall of the kitchen. "You sure took a big chance with that show in town." She opened a drawer, pulled out a folded newspaper, and handed it to Vicente. The caption on the largest advertisement on the page read:

Reward for Missing Circus Animals

The ad listed a zebra, lion, elephant, and orangutan with a substantial reward for information leading to their safe return. It ended with *The Malcolm Brothers Circus*.

Vicente's face sank.

Mabel shifted her weight on her crutches. "How will you get them from here to Port City with a reward on their head?"

"That's a good question—but I've wagered worse odds."

Mabel had a mischievous look in her eye. "I have an idea… Maybe you can stack the deck."

The corners of Vicente's mouth rounded into a half smile. "Hit me."—A reaction from his card playing days.

"Don't try to hide them—flaunt them."

Vicente tilted his head.

"Don't you see, instead of trying to hide the animals; put a sign on them that you are returning them to their owner for the reward! If anyone asks, you show them this—" She flaunted the newspaper ad next to her face. "—and off you go, no one the wiser!" She slapped the paper against her crutch, giddy with excitement.

Vicente smiled with conviction knowing that if anyone could pull off this bluff, it was him.

THIRTY-TWO

"What do you think?" Vicente asked, after explaining the idea while they hammered shingles onto the roof of the house. Jabari glanced at Vicente, unsure of what to say, and then, after another round of hammering, replied. "If you want them to trust you, you're going to have to trust them first."

"What do you mean?"

"I mean you lied to us about Louisa, and now you expect us to trust you with our lives? Trust has to go both ways," he said *matter-of-factly* while fitting another shingle onto the barn roof and hammering it into place.

"After all we've been through, you still don't trust me?" Vicente asked, hurt in his voice.

"I trust you, Vicente. But they have a higher standard of trust than me." Jabari hammered the point home, while he did the same to another nail: "I haven't been abused like them. If you're going to ask them to go along, you have to get them to trust you first!"

Later that evening, when the animals returned to the barn, Vicente wasted no time in calling them together. "I have some great news to share with everyone," Vicente declared to the animals in front of him, while O listened from above in the rafters. "But first, there's something I have to tell you."

Z and Ellie shifted, anticipating his next words, as Lefu eyed him.

Vicente took a deep breath. "I lied to you about Louisa

—" His voice quivered. "—She's my daughter... I'm sorry I lied." He waited a moment, and then looked at Jabari, awaiting a response from the animals.

"Why did you leave her?" asked Lefu. Jabari didn't hesitate and translated the question like it was his own.

Vicente looked down and his voice softened. "Because I was ashamed. I'd drank and gambled away everything I had and more—I owe people a lot of money... I couldn't face them." He lifted his head. "I hope you'll accept my apology." He looked at each animal. When Jabari said nothing, Vicente ran his fingers through his hair and took a deep breath. "The second thing I want to talk about is a plan to get you all to Port City. Now, before I tell you, I first need to let you know that the Malcolm Brothers have put out a reward for your return."

Lefu gave a low growl.

Vicente displayed the ad. "A very large reward...but this is going to help us."

Ellie's trunk curled downward, and Z's ears went back, and they both snorted in agitation. Jabari began to interpret, but Vicente cut him off. "Hear me out first." He raised his hand holding the ad. "Because they're looking for you, we can use this to our advantage. We can declare that we're returning you to the Malcolm Brothers for the reward. In fact, we put up a sign that says that we're returning you to them, and if anyone stops us, we can present the ad and be on our way, but not to the Malcolm Brothers, to Port City." Vicente gave a crafty smile and looked to Jabari for the animal's feedback.

Except for O, the animals snorted, growled, and brayed at each other, and after a minute of discussion amongst themselves, agreed. Jabari looked up to the rafters and caught O's eyes and received a quiet nod. "They understand and are good with the plan."

"Great." Vicente said, with partial relief. "One more thing. To make this work, Lefu will need to travel in a cage."

The roar from Lefu was thunderous and didn't require interpreting.

THE END OF THE CIRCUS

"Lefu, we can't have you walking loose in the streets," Vicente implored.

Another loud roar reverberated and Lefu paced around the barn in agitation.

Unafraid, Ellie reprimanded him. "Calm down, Lefu!"

"I am not going into another cage," He roared back, pacing the floor.

Z's ears popped up tall. "Lefu, I understand not wanting to do this, but think of what it means for all of us, including you— Besides, we can't stay here forever, and we can't go back. This is the only option we have."

Lefu slowed his pacing and came to a stop. He looked up in desperation at O above him in the rafters. O returned the look with an understanding, gentle smile, urging Lefu to be courageous once again. Lefu was ready to agree to the plan, when the barn door squeaked open.

"Is everything all right in here?" a voice said from the barn door.

Ellie, Z, and Lefu backed away from the unfamiliar person.

"It's all right, everyone," said Jabari to the animals in a tone that wouldn't betray his ability to speak with them. "This is Mabel, and she knows all about you. She's the one we've been telling you about."

Mabel stood at the door mesmerized by the sight in front of her.

Jabari waved her in. "It's okay, Mabel, come in and meet our friends."

Aided by her crutches, Mabel limped toward Jabari and Vicente, who stood together.

"I'd like you to meet Ellie." Jabari pointed to the elephant who took a step back and lowered her head. Jabari then turned to the zebra, "This is Z." Z's tail, ears, and nose twitched. Mabel looked at him with a smile. Jabari looked up to the ceiling. "This is O." Mabel's smile broadened as she eyed the wide face of the orange-haired creature, who glanced at her for a moment before looking away. "And this is Lefu, who I'm sure you heard,"

Jabari finished with a chuckle.

Overwhelmed, it took Mabel a moment before speaking. "They are wonderful! I'm glad to finally meet them after all this time."

Vicente touched Mabel's hand. "Thank you, Mabel, for letting us stay with you."

"You're welcome. I've been burning with curiosity but at first my wheelchair held me back, and then after seeing the reward, fear kept me away." Awe came upon her as she looked at them all again. "I wish I had come sooner. They are so beautiful."

Ellie blushed, and Z pulled his lips back in an awkward grin.

Mabel handed an envelope to Vicente. "I want to help you with some money for your journey… I've been saving this for a special occasion—" She smiled at the animals. "—and it doesn't get any more special than this."

Proud resistance was Vicente's first response, veiling his feelings of unworthiness. "We can't take that, Mabel."

Mabel straightened up and furrowed her brow. "You can and you will—you won't rob this old woman of the chance to do something good!"

Vicente understood her sentiment too well to resist. "Thank you." he said, as he and Jabari hugged her together.

"Thank you," said Jabari.

"You boys are welcome here anytime and let me know if there's anything more I can do for you." She turned and hobbled out of the barn, leaving the animals speechless until Ellie blew out a large breath. "She knew all along? … all this time, I've been afraid…"

Lefu's eyes widened. "Then we can stay!"

From the rafters, O's voice echoed against the high roof.

Vicente asked Jabari what he said, and Jabari translated: "Home is not about a roof. Home is about being where you belong."

Vicente felt a tug on his heart. "He's right. Let's get some sleep everyone… we have a lot of work to do." They settled in for the night and, except for Lefu, considered their journey and what the future might hold for them.

THIRTY-THREE

Delighted at the prospect of going home, Ellie was the first to rise. With her newfound freedom, she rousted everyone with a loud trumpet: "Up and at-em! She raised her trunk high with joyful enthusiasm. "We have a lot of work to do!" Shocked from their sleep, her human companions protested with moans and groans, with grunts and growls from Lefu and Z. O smiled at their comradery.

The group pulled out of their slumber, and the discussions began. They talked about what they needed and who would do what, then broke into teams. Ellie and O headed to the forest to collect small trees and branches for Lefu's cage, while Jabari and Vicente worked on repairing an old trailer that Mabel had given them. Z and Lefu simply enjoyed the day in the field and forest, as there was little they could do to help.

At the end of the first day, they'd gathered everything they needed, and the trailer was operable. By day two, they had half built the cage atop the trailer, and by the end of day three, they finished the door to the cage. Day four, they spent creating a harness for Z and Ellie to pull the trailer, and the fifth day was spent packing and provisioning supplies. Last, they affixed large 'Returning for Reward' signs on the front and back of the trailer, courtesy of Mabel. She also advised them on the best way to get to Port City, recommending roads with the least chance of being questioned or detained. To avoid being seen leaving Mabel's farm, they left in the black hours of the early morning. After a heartfelt goodbye to their host the prior evening, they awoke very early to begin their trip.

The journey into night was both exciting and frightening. They were moving forward, but they were also letting go of the safety and security of the farm. It had given them what they needed at the time—a safe place to heal and rest. They were going to need all the strength it had given them.

THIRTY-FOUR

The journey was easier than Vicente and Jabari had imagined. They answered questions by the few who couldn't contain their curiosity, and Vicente gave them enough information to satisfy them, but no more. Mabel's idea worked like a charm—most were content to accept the authority of a sign.

They rested and slept between towns, near rivers or ponds they found along the way. When they needed food, Jabari went ahead into the next town and bought what they required with the money Mabel gave them. He then waited outside of town for Vicente to arrive to load up, ensuring that their stops were as short as possible.

After several days of travel, while resting one afternoon at a secluded stop, Vicente addressed them. "We're only half a day away from Port City. We'll camp here tonight, but I need to go ahead and meet my friend to prepare for your arrival." The animals stirred in distress.

Jabari shuffled his feet. "You never said anything about leaving us and going ahead."

Vicente ran his fingers through his hair. "We can't go into the city without having somewhere for them to stay until we can leave again."

Jabari bit his lip and shoved his hands into his pockets. "What if someone tries to stop us?"

"You've seen how I handle the people that approach. Just do the same tomorrow if anyone asks." Vicente gave Jabari a knowing look. "You can do this." He waited for Jabari to show any sign of acceptance, but none came. "I'm asking you to trust me." He looked at Jabari and then at each animal. "Leave at noon tomorrow. I'll meet you tomorrow evening on the main road into town, and I'll join you from there." Vicente snatched a few bread buns and stuffed them into his pockets. "I have to go now if I'm going to get there before dark." He headed toward the road, hurrying toward their hopes.

"I don't trust him," growled Lefu from his cage.

Jabari sighed. "We don't have a choice."

"Hmm," said Ellie.

Z scuffed the ground with his hoof. "If he wanted to cross us, why would he go to all the trouble to get us here?"

"What do you think, O?" Jabari asked his wise friend.

O lay sprawled out with his arms above his head, soothing his back on the cool grass, and spoke to the sky, "Trust not about Vicente. Trust about you." He allowed the thought to settle, then added, "Better to choose trust. Not fear."

THIRTY-FIVE

"Won any bets lately, amigo?" Vicente asked. The man seated in the café turned to see the speaker, although the wide smile on his face showed that he knew who it was. The enormous man ignored his table company and shot up from his stool and greeted the speaker, "My friend!" he said in a thick, gruff French Moroccan accent. He wrapped his arms around Vicente "How great to see you!"

Older than Vicente by a decade, he had thick black hair, a wide, powerful face, a heavy beard, and thick eyebrows. Unable to wrap his arms around the large man, Vicente slapped his back in greeting, after which they looked at each other for a moment to take in each other's presence.

"You look good, Vicente," said the man, his massive hand on Vicente's shoulder.

The enthusiasm of his greeting warmed Vicente. "You too, Captain!"

"How long has it been?" asked the captain.

"Too long… it's great to see you again."

"So good to see you, Vicente…How did you find me?"

"I asked around the wharf and was told you might be here."

"You're lucky you caught me; I sail tomorrow for Africa."

Vicente gave a smile that curled up one side of his face. "Luck seems to have my back of late."

THE END OF THE CIRCUS

The captain squeezed Vicente's shoulder. "You must join me tonight!"

"Okay," Vicente said, not knowing what the offer entailed, only that he needed his friend's help.

"What brings you here? —" He motioned to the bartender. "—First things first! A drink for my friend!"

Vicente motioned 'no' with his hands to the bartender. "I quit drinking, Captain; none for me, but thank you."

The captain took a moment to reconcile this new information with his enthusiasm for sharing a drink and came to his friend's support. "Good for you, Vicente!" His large hand patted his shoulder. "I should give this stuff up too," he said with a coarse chuckle of solidarity.

"Can we talk somewhere privately?" Vicente asked in a thoughtful tone.

The captain eyed him with both concern and intrigue; he'd never seen his friend so serious. "Yes, of course," he said. "Follow me." The captain rose from his chair, threw money on the table, shot back the balance of his drink, put on his captain's hat, and without saying goodbye to his companions, led Vicente out the door. His friends at the table looked on in astonishment at how the captain regarded this man.

The pair walked to the wharf where the captain unlocked a gate, then locked it behind them again. They then made their way to an old retrofitted fishing boat. It had the lingering odors of fish and fuel and Vicente repulsed as they boarded. The captain led him to his quarters and seated Vicente at his desk, facing the captain who wasted no time in starting the conversation. "How can I help you, my good friend?"

Vicente took a deep breath, then told him their story, and what he wanted from the captain.

When he'd finished, the captain leaned into him, gave a wink and a wry smile. "Lucky for you, my friend, my boat has difficulties and won't be able to sail until the day after tomorrow."

Relieved, Vicente slumped in his chair. "Thank you,

Captain."

The captain spread his arms wide, as though offering his kingdom. "Anything you ask, my friend… but you already knew that."

THIRTY-SIX

Jabari couldn't sleep as he considered the next day. He was anxious to be responsible for the animals without Vicente, and, he was excited at the thought of returning home. He peered into the night sky and saw the stars, and they reminded him of the words his mother had said to him often as a child:

'They are there to remind you of the infinite possibilities, and that the power that created this grandness, is surely able to help you.'

He rarely thought of the words his mother had spoken to him. Rather, he'd become accustomed to looking to the sky whenever he was unsure, or in need. He remembered how he'd looked to the sky on the night of the fire when he saved his friends, and again on their first day together when he was unsure of what would become of them. Now, here again, he looked up, and he considered O's words from earlier that day. He turned his head toward his friend resting on the sleeping platform atop Lefu's cage beside him. "O, are you awake?"

"Yes."

"What you said about trust earlier today… does it apply to things you can't see?" He waited a moment for O to reply.

"What you mean, Jabari?"

Jabari shared his mother's wisdom and awaited his teachers reply.

"Your mother wise…" He stretched his long arms above him. "…When you trust Vicente, was because you *know* you trust, or because you see enough good for trust?"

Jabari recalled the day in the tree. "I didn't *know* I could trust him, but I sensed that he was good."

"It same with no-see," said O. "We not know unseen. But see enough good—" He looked up at the stars and across the fields. "—to choose trust."

Jabari considered O's words while he gazed at the stars in the majestic silence of the sky. He absorbed the immensity and the possibilities, and he decided to trust. He then closed his eyes and drifted asleep.

Jabari and the animals awoke to the sounds of birds chirping in the brisk fall air. After he fed the animals, the rest of the morning crept by as they followed Vicente's instruction to wait until noon before leaving. When it was time, Jabari collected the blankets, folded them, and put them on the cart. After opening the cage and locking in Lefu, he harnessed Ellie and Z to the wagon, and waited for O to join him on the bench. With a nod to Ellie and Z, they departed.

The early afternoon of the trip passed in quiet, and this comforted Jabari. He was thinking he might not have to speak to anyone, but as they came closer to the city, there were more homes and in mid-morning, a man, dressed in a fine suit, approached them from the front, walking along the side of the road. He stood with his shoulders back, head held high. He was well-groomed, light skinned, and carried himself with an air of self-importance. Jabari tensed and tightened his grip on the reins, to the notice of O beside him.

"What is the manner of this!" said the man, his polished English voice dripping with authority and judgment.

Jabari's anxiety spiked; his mind went blank and his palms sweat.

Ellie and Z looked back at Jabari for direction.

"Keep move," whispered O. He placed a hand on Jabari's thigh and brought him back to the moment.

Jabari glanced at O and without thought, flicked the reigns; Ellie and Z continued. The man glowered at Jabari and his face went hot. "I said, what is the manner of this!"

A rush of fear shot through Jabari's body and his mind searched in vain for something to grasp. He glanced up at the sky in desperation but there were no stars. He tried to recall the words that Vicente had used, but he could not find them. He felt like a frightened, helpless child—like the day the uniformed men came for his father.

The man stepped closer to the road, as though intending to stand in their way to stop them. Jabari froze.

"Remember stars." said O, placing a hand on Jabari's thigh again.

Jabari's mother's words floated through him, and with it, strength he did not know he possessed, billowed up from his belly. It formed bubbles in his throat that he couldn't contain, and his mouth formed words he could feel, but didn't understand. It was as though someone or something else was trying to speak through him, yet he sensed it was part of him. He spoke with authority and kept his gaze on the road, without ever looking at the man. "Neither I, nor these animals are accountable to you! We are free as we are meant to be!"

The confident man stopped walking, lost his stiffness, and became speechless as they passed him. Not only had he not expected such an articulate response, but there was an authority and power in the words of the youthful man atop the cart. Determined not to be overcome, the man opened his mouth to speak again, when Lefu roared and lunged toward him, rattling and tilting the improvised cage. Terrified, the man jumped back and stepped away from the cart. Shaken, he gulped his unspoken words in fear.

Jabari looked straight ahead as the cart continued. "What's he doing? Is he following us?" he whispered to O.

O looked back over his shoulder and eyed up the man, who returned and held his look, but not for long. As Jabari's words were more powerful, so was O's deep and penetrating gaze; like all great creatures can, he saw the man for who he was, and reflected it back to him. Upon seeing himself, the man averted his eyes, slunk, and walked away. "He go," said O.

Jabari's mouth dropped open. "I can't believe what I said."

"You do good." said O

"Where did that even come from?"

O pointed to his stomach with a smile. "Magic place."

"I think it was the star makers," said Jabari.

"Same-same, but different," said O.

O put his hand on Jabari's shoulder to the sounds of Ellie, Z, and Lefu's hoots, hurrahs and hollers in the form of trumpets, braying, and roars.

THIRTY-SEVEN

Jabari was never so confident as he drove that final stretch into Port City. He sat erect with his head held high, with a lingering smile from the memory of his encounter with the arrogant man. Even though he was ready and eager to practice his newfound confidence, much to his disappointment, no one approached the cart or asked questions.

They didn't see Vicente on the approach to the city as they'd expected, but not knowing where on the road he planned to meet them, they edged forward. Unsure and unaccustomed to the sights and sounds of the city, Ellie halted. "Where's Vicente?"

Jabari snapped the reins. "He said he'd be here on the road into the city; we need to keep going until we see him."

Ellie stepped forward again. "What if he doesn't show up?"

"He'll be here," said Jabari, then turned to O with his eyebrows raised and a questioning look on his face. The orangutan smiled.

They continued for some time at a very slow pace and Jabari's confidence wavered. He was considering his options when an enormous man approached. "You must be Jabari. I am the Captain, a good friend of Vicente's. He asked me to meet you here." Jabari pulled on the reins and Ellie and Z stopped.

Although the words comforted Jabari, Vicente's absence distressed him. "Where's Vicente?" he asked with a healthy dose of suspicion.

Lefu growled a low rumble from the cage. "This wasn't what Vicente told us!"

The captain ignored Jabari's question. "We have to get to the port."

A remnant of Jabari's newfound confidence coursed through his veins. "I demand you tell me where Vicente is!"

The captain turned and glowered at the insubordinate young man.

Jabari held his gaze, though his stomach turned, and he was afraid of what might happen next.

The captain relaxed his stance. "He told me you were brave." then chuckled at Jabari's courage. "Vicente asked me to meet you because he had arrangements to make. He asked me to take you to the port to sail tomorrow. I don't know anything else. Do you want to go home? Or should I leave you here?"

Jabari eyed the gathering crowd trying to get a closer look at the animals.

Lefu growled. "Don't trust him."

"We don't have a choice," said Jabari, but the captain assumed Jabari was speaking to him.

"Okay, follow me," said the captain with a puzzled look on his face. He led them down a side street, away from the busy thoroughfare. The sun was getting low in the sky and they zigged and zagged as they descended; alternating between shadows and light and Jabari wondered which of the two would be their fate. They soon found themselves on flat land again and made their way to a gated wharf. The captain produced a key, opened the gate, beckoned them through, and locked it behind them.

Excited to be going home, Ellie and Z pranced toward a large boat waiting at the dock. But before they got there, the captain stopped opposite it at the gate of a large compound with a high fence topped with barbed wire. "You will stay here until we sail tomorrow." He extracted a key from his pocket and unlocked the gate.

Illuminated by a lamppost, with a single light atop it, a

sign on the fence, read *Rental Storage.*

The captain nodded toward the far corner of the compound. "Food and water are there." He then swung the gate open wide and waited for them to enter.

Jabari sensed the animal's reluctance at being caged for the first time since leaving the circus, and he was uncomfortable going forward. "This one is up to you."

The captain raised an eyebrow. "Who are you talking to?"

"The animals."

The captain pursed his lips and tapped his foot on the ground. "What are you waiting for!"

"For them to answer," said Jabari.

The captain scowled and lowered his head, holding his breath. He then looked up to say something more when Z Brayed, Ellie trumpeted, and Lefu roared.

Jabari ignored their arguments and protests. "*You* have to decide."

"Yes, for me," said Ellie.

"Me too" said Z.

"Yes," said O.

"No," said Lefu, as he paced in circles in his cage atop the cart.

Jabari dropped his head in despair, then lifted it. "We have a problem… Captain, sir; the lion does not want to go into the compound."

The captain looked at Jabari. "I am here to do what my friend asked me to. No more, no less, but if you don't wait here, I will fail my friend. That is not something I will do. So, what do you want me to do?"

"Ask him why we can't wait on the boat," Lefu said.

"Why can't we go on the boat?" asked Jabari.

"Because Vicente said for you to spend the night here. All I know is that he has done a lot to help you—he does that well."

"Assuming the animals agree to go in…I want the key." said Jabari.

The captain looked at Jabari with his patience running

thin. He was the one who gave orders. "I can't do that."

Jabari's eyes widened. "What do you mean, you can't do that!"

The captain lowered his head as he spoke. "Vicente asked me to keep the key."

Jabari's eyes went hot and narrowed. "What!"

Ellie and Z stirred, and Lefu roared.

Jabari put out his arm, palm up. "I am not going in without the key!"

Exasperated, the captain reached into his pocket, fumbled around and handed Jabari a key.

Jabari turned back from atop the bench. "Lefu, we have the key. Do you want me to let you run these streets by yourself?" He fixed his eyes on Lefu. "We all made our decision a long time ago—we aren't turning back."

"Come on, Lefu; you're part of us," said Ellie.

Lefu stopped pacing, "If this turns out to be something else, I swear I'll kill him." He followed up with a roar.

Ellie rolled her eyes, flared her ears out wide. "We know, Lefu—It's your solution to everything."

Lefu shot a glare at Ellie, but before another exchange was possible, Jabari jumped in, speaking to the captain, "We're good!" He snapped the reins, and Ellie and Z moved forward.

They halted in the middle of the compound when the haunting sounds of chains clanking over steel, followed by the clicking of the lock, resounded behind them. A tingle ran down Lefu's tail, and the small hairs on Ellie's and Z's back rose. The captain's footsteps echoed away in the silence of the empty wharf, as he walked back toward the wharf gate and disappeared into the darkness.

THIRTY-EIGHT

Jabari stepped down from the cart, undid Ellie and Z from their harnesses, and opened Lefu's cage. He then made his way to the corner of the compound and lifted a tarpaulin, revealing baskets of food. Although it was comforting, a foreboding settled upon them. Lefu snapped up a piece of meat and gulped it down. "Our last supper—may as well enjoy it!"

Jabari ignored Lefu, and as the others ate, he snatched two apples from a basket, and walked back to the cart. He climbed back up and handed an apple to O and took a bite from the other. After finishing his mouthful, he stared at the ground in front of him. "I trusted him," he said with despair. "Did I make a mistake?"

O looked at him with his penetrating gaze. "You only make mistake when no learn. When choose learn, no mistake, only wiser or succeed."

Jabari took another bite from his apple and chewed on both O's words and the fruit. "I hope I don't get wiser tonight."

O put his hand on Jabari's shoulder. "You already wise, but I hope so, too." O took a large bite from his apple.

It was colder near the ocean, and Jabari prepared for the night. He dragged the tarp that had covered the food and unfolded it to form a temporary sleeping area for the animals. He then brought blankets from the cart, placed them on Lefu, and Z, with a re-assuring look, and then, with a strained smile, threw one atop Ellie.

Ellie smiled a thank you with sad eyes. "Will you sing to

us, like you did in the circus?"

Jabari fidgeted with his satchel. "Why do you want me to do that?"

"Because it made me feel so good."

Z paced nearby and added to the discussion: "I have to admit it made me feel good, too…" He shivered from the cool ocean air. "…I think we could use some of that right now."

"What would you like me to sing?"

Ellie raised her trunk and placed it on Jabari's shoulder. "It doesn't matter; it's your voice that does it."

Jabari was encouraged and it confirmed that his singing indeed, comforted the animals. Realizing that he too, could use some solace, he sang a gentle tune from his childhood. His voice was ethereal and warm, and it echoed throughout the wharf as if an angelic choir backed him. It touched their hearts, and a peaceful calm settled them.

Ellie exhaled an emotional sigh from her trunk. "Thank you." She took a deep breath. "That was beautiful," she said with a lilt, then exhaled.

He gave her a serene smile. "You're welcome."

Calm and ready for sleep, Z made his way to the tarp, his hooves echoing throughout the wharf. When he reached it, the echo of his steps continued for a moment, but when they didn't stop, he looked at his hooves to be sure, and then at everyone else's feet. His intrigued listening caught the groups attention, and they realized that someone was walking toward the wharf gate. The lamppost allowed them to be seen, but they couldn't see beyond its light. Hearing only muffled speech, they remained still, peering into the darkness for any clue as to who was there, and what they were doing.

❋ ❋ ❋

"Did you bring the reward money?" said the captain.

"First the animals," said the younger Malcolm brother.

The captain motioned to them under the light. "Over

there; in the compound."

The elder Malcolm responded as he eyed the animals up with satisfaction. "I see, but we don't have them yet."

The captain pulled a piece of paper from his pocket. "Ah, but you do. Here's the rental agreement for the compound."

He passed it through the gap in the wharf gate between the lock and chains, to the waiting hand of Malcolm Sr. "What do we need this for?"

"To get them in the morning." The captain pointed to the compound's sign. "Rental Storage, see?"

Malcolm Jr's face twisted. "In the morning?"

The older brother puffed his chest. "We came here to collect them as promised by the old woman."

"And you have them." The captain pulled a key from his pocket and pointed it at the paper. "This is the key for the rental compound".

Malcolm Junior took the agreement from his brother and lit a match to read it. The flame illuminated both the paper and his face.

❋ ❋ ❋

Z's neck stiffened and a large vein on his forehead pulsed. The face in the flame was imprinted on him like none other. "It's Malcolm Junior!" he said wide eyed. "The captain has sold us out!"

Lefu's ears retreated and his jowls tightened. Enraged, he roared, ran toward the voices and jumped high against the fence. His body smashed into the links and he pushed his claws through them in a feeble attempt to support his weight. He then fell to the ground, only to throw himself back against the fence. He did this repeatedly with no awareness of what he was doing to himself.

Malcolm Sr. tilted his head back and snickered at the lion. "He hasn't changed a bit."

Z brayed, "Jabari, get us out of here!" Jabari jumped, jolted out of his entrancement with Lefu and reached into his satchel, grabbed the key and raced to the gate. He had a sense of déjà vu as he lifted the lock and chain and tried to insert the key, first one way, then the other. The animals pressed against him awaiting escape.

Ellie waved her ears. "Hurry, Jabari!"

Jabari's pressed his lips together, then shook his head in frustration before his eyes went hot. "IT DOESN'T FIT!"

Z's nose was over Jabari's shoulder. "What do you mean it doesn't fit!"

Jabari slammed his hands against the links "The key doesn't fit the lock!" Then he dropped his head against the fence. "He tricked us!"

Z's ears fell, and Ellie's lay flat, as her entire body slouched. Their worst fears had come upon them.

❋ ❋ ❋

"We'll pay you in the morning, when we collect them," said the younger, his nose high, glancing at the agreement dismissively. The captain snatched the agreement out of his hand, folded it, and stuffed it back into his pocket. He stared at the brothers. "I sail before dawn. Either I sail with the animals, or I sail with the reward money."

"Hold on a moment," said the elder brother. "Let me look at that again." He held his hand open, awaiting the document.

The captain passed it to the elder brother, who lit another match and scanned it until the matchstick burned to his fingers. He blew out the match. "Why can't we get them now?"

The captain folded his arms. "Because this gate is locked for the night and the harbor master won't unlock it 'til morning and I'll be gone before dawn. Take it or leave it," he added with a shrug.

The elder brother looked back at the compound and the young man with the group of animals at the gate. "And what are we to do with the boy?"

"Consider him a bonus," said the captain, with a flick of his hand.

Malcolm Jr. looked at his brother and, as siblings often do, understood each other without words. "Agreed." said the eldest. He opened his vest and pulled a large envelope from his jacket pocket. He cautiously handed it to the captain with his left hand, in exchange for the agreement and key, into his right.

The captain held the envelope open to the dim moonlight and fanned through the bills with his thumb. He then stowed the envelope in his pocket. With an abrupt nod, he said "Goodnight," then turned and walked away from the gate as the brothers did the same.

Jabari, O, Ellie, Z, and Lefu stood in a row at the compound fence, with the lamppost casting their shadows onto the wooden pier. In stunned silence, they watched the captain trample over their silhouettes, and onto his boat.

THIRTY-NINE

"Will it ever end?" said Ellie in disbelief as they left the fence and made their way to the tarp.

They were cold, tired after their many days of walking and, above all, disheartened. They considered what had happened and what it meant for them. Returning to the circus was incomprehensible after having been free for so long. They were not the same creatures who'd left the circus; they discovered that they were much more than the roles they'd taken. Having tasted freedom, the thought of returning with this knowing was unbearable—worse than never having left.

Lefu made his way to a corner of the tarp and lay down, but sleep wasn't a consideration for the others.

"I can't go back," said Z to his elephant friend.

Ellie looked at him with a half-smile. "I never thought I'd hear those words from the soldier I used to know."

"Me neither…" Z opened his mouth again but struggled to find the words. "… the mask I wore to survive is gone…and I can't put it back on."

Ellie put her trunk on his neck and pet him. "Mine too."

Z smiled at the comfort. "You know what's weird. I spent my life in fear, but this—not wanting to go back—isn't fear. I don't know what it means. All I know is that I can't go back."

Downcast, Jabari climbed onto the cart bench near O, who had climbed atop Lefu's cage to prepare for the night. Upon seeing his sadness, O offered words of comfort: "No be sad. You make right choice, Jabari."

Jabari lay on his back. Clouds were drifting in the night sky, hiding and revealing the moon and stars. "I failed them." His eyes went moist. "I thought I was helping but it would have been better if they'd never come with me."

O also lay on his back, arms overhead, watching the night sky, and after a few more clouds drifted by, he turned to his young friend. "You not what happen in life, Jabari."

Jabari shifted uncomfortably. He wasn't in the mood for O's wisdom, but for the love and respect he held for his good friend, he restrained himself.

O ignored Jabari's silence. "We here for big reason. Sometime hard to see." O looked around and gestured to the animals with his lengthy arm. "Angry lion, hurt elephant, soldier zebra—" He gazed and pointed at Jabari. "—fatherless son." Jabari swallowed as O continued. "We choose who we be this life to learn who we really are. Inside, we perfect, magical…complete. No add nothing. No takeaway nothing. What happen not matter." He paused again as the sky caught his attention, revealing itself in fresh ways. "Magic part inside perfect but get made better. It grow like flower. Always perfect but grow more beautiful. Circus a gift to give you choice."

Though stuck in his sadness and not in agreement, Jabari didn't protest.

O turned and looked at Jabari again. "Outcome, you no control. Choice you control. You make right choice, Jabari." O emphasized each word and counted them on his dark fingers. "You choose courage, faith, friendship, love. Not outcome that matter, what you choose matter."

Jabari found it hard to accept O's words. He wanted to be sad and responsible—To loathe himself and wallow in self-judgement—punishment he thought he deserved. Although part of him knew O was right, he thought it a betrayal to his friends to let himself off the hook. Thoughts of what might happen to him and his friends also distracted him. Would he be accused of burning the circus and stealing the animals? Would he go to jail? He was considering these questions when the sound of approaching footsteps interrupted him. *Vicente?* Jabari lifted his head, but to his disappointment, it was the Captain coming toward them.

"Jabari, it's time to go," said the captain from the other side of the compound fence.

Jabari jumped from the trailer and marched to the gate; his eyes fiery. "We saw you with the Malcolm Brothers!"

"Yes," he said, puffing himself up with pride.

Ellie and Z looked at one another, bewildered.

Jabari's nostrils flared. "We aren't going anywhere with you!"

The captain grimaced. "I thought you want to go home?"

"Of course, we want to go home!"

"Then you must get on the boat," the captain said in the manner of one urging a child.

Jabari scowled at the captain. "What deal did you make with the Malcolm Brothers!"

The captain gave a cunning smile. "I traded you for the reward money."

Jabari stared at him, speechless at the man's brazen confession. His anger rose and he was about to tear into him, when the seaman's smile broadened, "That is, as long as you are still here in the morning."

A clang came from the wharf gate, followed by footsteps running in the darkness. Vicente appeared in the compound light and stood next to the captain.

Jabari's eyes widened at the sight of his friend.

Vicente was winded. "They're at their hotel… I followed them to be sure we're alone," Vicente said to the captain between breaths, before blurting in a continuous stream, "Let's open this gate and get them loaded. Jabari, are you okay? How is everyone?"

The captain reached into his pocket and produced a key, unlocked the padlock and swung open the compound gate.

Jabari ran to his friend and threw his arms around him.

Vicente smiled at Jabari's relief. "You didn't think I'd left you, did you?"

Jabari released his hold and looked at Vicente, dazed. "Why didn't you show up as planned?"

"I'm sorry, Jabari. It took so much longer than I thought to get the storage area and the food for the trip arranged." He nodded at the captain. "So, I asked my friend the captain to help. Mabel arranged to get the Malcolm Brothers to their hotel, and once I knew you were here, I sent them a message to meet the captain."

Jabari's mouth fell open. "*You* brought the Malcolm Brothers!"

Vicente put his hands on Jabari's shoulders. "To pay the captain to take you home—Why waste the reward money?" Vicente said with a crooked smile. "Besides, they had it coming."

Jabari's eyes narrowed. "Why didn't you tell us?"

Vicente motioned to the animals as he spoke. "Because their trust was hanging by a thread and I wasn't sure they'd agree.

The realization sunk in and Jabari's countenance shifted as the burden he carried fell from him. He turned to the animals who, except for Lefu, stood and stared at the open gate. With a full smile and his eyes sparkling with excitement, Jabari shouted: "We're going home!" He ran past the cart, slapped its side, and shot O a thankful look, then continued to the tarp where he announced the news to Lefu.

"You don't have to tell us twice," Ellie said as she and Z stepped out and onto the wharf.

"Lefu, come on!" said Jabari, but Lefu slept. Jabari approached him from his back and nudged him. "Wake up, Lefu," but the lion didn't respond. He then shook him with increasing vigor. "Lefu, wake up!" He shook him with all his strength, but the lion didn't stir. Jabari turned his head back to the others. "Something's wrong with Lefu!"

Vicente ran into the compound followed by the captain, sauntering.

Jabari's voice crackled. "He won't wake up!"

"That's because I added something to his meat," said the Captain matter-of-factly.

Jabari's anger rose. "What!"

The captain waived a hand, dismissively. "He'll be fine—He's sleeping. He won't wake up until we're long gone."

Jabari shook his head in disbelief. "Why would you do that?"

The captain pointed to the scar on Vicente's neck. "Because of that."

Vicente's pitch went high. "I told you why he did that, Captain." The captain shrugged.

Jabari stroked Lefu's body. "He wouldn't hurt anyone he trusts."

Jabari glared up at the captain. "You definitely aren't one of them now!"

❋ ❋ ❋

The boarding was more difficult than Vicente and the captain had anticipated. Carrying a limp and unconscious lion down a flight of stairs was an arduous task and lifting Ellie and Z by hoist in the dark of night, though different, was also challenging. But after some hard work, Z and Ellie found themselves in cargo holds below openings in the ship's deck, with Lefu alone in a lower berth, and O in a cage near Jabari's bunk. But their quarters were far less pleasant than the animals had expected; the remnant smell of fish was nauseating and overwhelming to their fined tuned senses.

With their work complete, Vicente realized it was time to say goodbye. Standing on the deck of the boat, he gazed at the captain. "Thank you so much for everything you've done."

"I'm the thankful one, my friend." A rare touch of emotion welled in him. "I owe you my life. This is the least I can do."

Vicente thought 'the least' was referring to his help, but the captain reached into his pocket and pulled out the envelope he'd placed there earlier. "This is for you. I hope it balances the scales."

Vicente shook his head and protested: "No, no, no… I can't take that."

But the captain stopped him short. "Take it for Louisa." He grabbed Vicente's right hand and forced the envelope into it. "Besides, after the expenses for food for the journey, there's not much left," he added with a smile.

Vicente eyed the large envelope and doubted the captain took any of the money. With gratitude forming in his eyes, he slowly looked up, then beamed, before throwing his arms around his old friend. "Thank you!" He slapped the captain's back with his free hand. "Thank you," he repeated, in a soft tone as he realized what this gift meant to him. Until that moment, Vicente was going to return to Louisa and face the worst; shame and rejection of family and friends, with no plan for compensation. He blew out a breath of relief and shook his head as he recalled O's message at the farm. *The universe always supports the highest intentions of the heart.*

He turned to Jabari and embraced him. "Gracias for believing in me. Your mission and faith in me gave me the purpose I needed."

"You didn't give me much of a choice." Jabari said laughing, as they pulled back from their embrace. "Thank you for all your help. I couldn't have done this without you."

Vicente returned the smile, his voice still carrying a light raspy reminder of Lefu's claw. "Could have, and would have, Amigo. You are stronger than you know." He then extracted a large section of bills from the envelope and handed them to Jabari. "You will need this for transport when you get to the coast."

Jabari's mouth went slack and he slapped Vicente's shoulder. He had given little thought to the lengthy journey to the savannah and was surprised by both the offer and the need. "Thank you, Vicente," he said, his face turning solemn. "I will miss you."

"You too, amigo," said Vicente.

Vicente turned his attention to O, standing next to Jabari. "Gracias Amigo for helping me face my fears."

O gazed at him and smiled. "Fear only real when we let it be." Vicente nodded and then looked at Z and Ellie in their holds. "I will tell marvelous stories to my Louisa about all of you!" He paused, reminiscing while looking each one in the eye. "...Please tell Lefu that I'll miss him, and that I wish I had a chance to say adios." He then gave a last nod to the captain, turned and left the ship.

Jabari, O, and the captain watched as he walked away and past the light of the compound. When they could see him no more, they listened to his footsteps in the darkness, until the clang of the gate echoed farewell.

FORTY

Lefu

"Don't go too far," the lioness admonished her son as he hunted grasshoppers in the tall summer grass nearby. He was a fun-loving cub, whose infectious delight at the wonders he experienced in his first few months, had led to the moniker Cheka, meaning laughter.

Every day was a new adventure for him, and every sight and sound a fresh opportunity to explore. The marvel of the world unfolded to him with joy, and he laughed at every new discovery. Grasses and light, animals and insects, all intertwined and interacted, often leaving him wide-eyed with surprise, followed by hearty laughter, and an insatiable curiosity for more. His investigation of the world around him this morning drew him further and further from the safety of his mother. The grasshoppers hopped, and with each leap, Cheka bounded toward them, until he caught sight of his father, ahead in the distance.

Practicing his best hunting crawl, he lowered his body and drifted, paw in front of paw, toward him. But as he moved, so did his father. Some time passed before Cheka realized that he didn't know where he was, or where his mother was, but he was comforted that he was only a scant distance from his father. He couldn't contain the excitement that whirled inside him as he imagined himself jumping up to the surprise of his father—*the new great hunter in his pride!* He snickered to himself, ready to jump, when his father's booming roar caused him to shudder. Cheka thought he'd been discovered and was being chastised for being away from his mother, but that illusion soon vanished, as the cause of his father's bellows became clear.

Through the grass, he saw a group of men enclosing his father from all directions—men with hats and long sticks. Several of them held ropes and nets as they enclosed him—his father had nowhere to go. Cheka wished he'd listened to his mother to stay close. *Grasshoppers!* He laid low in the grass and didn't move for fear.

The men drew closer, shouting, taunting, and prodding their sticks toward his father, that left the lion on guard from all sides at once. They closed him within their circle. It appeared to Cheka that they would soon be upon him when his father pounced atop one man, and a thunderous sound split the sky. Terrified, and deafened from the blast, Cheka pressed himself flat against the ground, shivering. When he lifted his head to peak through the upper grasses, his father was limp and lifeless.

Unable to hear his own whimpers of distress, Cheka drew the attention of one of the light-skinned men. "What do we have here?" He reached for Cheka and picked him up by the scruff. He then carried him to an enormous cage, bragging and sniggering as he walked. "Not what we expected, but we got a lion!"

Cheka looked upon the bloody, languid body of his father through the bars of the cage, buried his face in his paws, and cried.

His journey in the cage was frightening and lonely. He longed to be with his mother again, to play in the tall grass and, most of all, to laugh with his father. The men carted him from unknown place, to unknown place: from savannah, to village, to forest, to port, and lastly to the bowels of a ship. There he spent many days and nights listening to the chug of the boat engine, taking him far away from his pride, and the only home he ever knew.

FORTY-ONE

Lefu pried open one eye and then the other. Chug, chug, chug, echoed from below. His mouth was dry, his body ached, and his mind was sluggish. What's going on? The boat continued to chug below him. He tried to discern if he was dreaming of his past or living it again. He struggled to lift himself, then shook his head to clear it. What happened?

He remembered being exhausted after eating the food left for him by the captain. *Drugged!* Lefu began pacing his cage, trying to make sense of it. *Why would that captain drug me? To sell me?* "Not again!" he roared.

His past and present exploded in an emotional fusion, and the fear that he'd repressed for so many years, thrust up in his stomach and overtook his weakened mind. He hadn't been able to manage this fear as a cub and was ill prepared to manage it now that he believed—fueled by his imagination—that it was happening again. His walk shifted from slow and thoughtful, to an aggressive prowl, as the negative energy built in him. *Not this time...* he thought to himself *...not this time.*

FORTY-TWO

Tending to the animals again, Jabari was reliving his days in the circus. The animals, however, found the journey difficult and long, as they waited in the isolation of their dim, damp, and foul compartments. To comfort them and distract them from the unpleasant quarters aboard the ship, Jabari often sang to them as he cleaned their stalls, fed and watered them. He also asked them questions about going home, and what they were looking forward to.

They eagerly shared, except Lefu, who alone in the lower berth, offered no response. In fact, he had very little to say since he awoke aboard the ship. Jabari had tried to tell him on many occasions what Vicente had done for them, or how the captain had helped them, but before he could explain, Lefu stopped Jabari mid-sentence with a roar that ended the conversation. His only words were to demand that he be let out of his cage. "You know I can't do that," replied Jabari each time, having explained to Lefu that the captain was clear that no animal was to roam freely on the ship.

Despite these circumstances, Jabari found the voyage meaningful and comforting. Unlike at the farm, he spent most of his time with the animals, and his friendship deepened with all of them, but most of all, with O. The orangutan had a calming presence for those who would accept it, but something beyond this touched Jabari; he had become the father Jabari had lost. Jabari spent many days and nights sharing and asking questions of the wise man of the forest; often sneaking O out of his cage to breathe fresh air and watch the stars from atop the ship.

One sleepless night, troubled by another sharp encounter with Lefu that day, Jabari shared his frustration with O. "I don't understand Lefu. He's so angry." Jabari shook his head and stared into the sky, watching the clouds pass before the moonlight.

"You no have to understand."

Jabari frowned. "Why does he have to be so difficult?"

"He go through much; he just no remember."

"Remember what?"

The boat rocked in a gentle rhythm, as its bow broke through the water.

"We here to remember who we are, Jabari."

Jabari threw his head back and rolled his eyes. "Then Lefu's totally forgotten."

O smiled with kind eyes. "No try understand. Love and accept better. Understand no lead to love—but love always lead to understand."

Jabari pursed his lips and took a breath.

O turned his large, warm eyes to him. "Maybe if you lose not only father, but mother, family, and home, you be angry too."

Jabari furrowed his brow and shook his head sideways. "I could never be so hateful!"

"No judge, Jabari; it test you." Jabari gave a dismissive look.

O put a hand on Jabari's leg. "Better to love. Love help him remember. Only hope for all is love."

Jabari thought for a few moments as he scratched at the flaking paint of the ship. "It's hard to accept someone who's so angry."

"Yes, but make reward better."

Jabari gave a crooked smile. "In that case, I look forward to being rich."

O smiled back. "You already *very* rich."

The bow broke another wave and they lay back and

watched the clouds paint the sky anew.

FORTY-THREE

Like Jabari, Lefu was also reliving his days in the circus; he once again found himself caged, his anger burning, biding his time, and dreaming of retaliation. The torment of the ship's isolation provoked his darkened imagination, and he obsessed about overtaking the captain. Cutting him down with his razor-sharp claws and standing atop his body roaring, became his vision of vengeance. He replayed the scene incessantly, thinking of little else during his waking hours.

Falling asleep and waking up however, were different matters. When the guard of his mind lowered its defenses, the chug of the ship's engine pulled him back to a memory he could not suppress. It took him a long time to sleep, and when he did, even his dreams were painful and frightening reminders, only to wake again to the chug of the ship's engines. Try as he might to quell the emotions of his childhood, the rhythm of the engines tormented the shivering and frightened cub deep inside him.

Lefu had never felt his pain so acutely. Isolated, exhausted from lack of sleep and afraid, his boiling rage evaporated what remained of his conscience. He no longer cared about anything or anyone—not even what might happen to him. He became fully convinced that somehow, this act—this one singular act—would balance the scales of a lifetime of injustice. Unlike with Vicente, this time he wouldn't forgive.

Without conscience, he resolved to act, but realized if he waited for their arrival on shore, the captain might steal his opportunity. Escaping the cage was his only option, *but how*?

While considering the thought, a mouse squeaked at the corner of the cage, and made its way across the floor, over and under bits of straw. Lefu watched motionless until it was within reach, then struck. He raised his paw to reveal the lifeless, skewered mouse and examined it with morbid satisfaction. Retracting his claws, the mouse fell to the floor, and his eyes became intense. Maintaining focus on his paw, he protracted his claws again, retracted them, then like a machine, repeated the motion several times.

    A gleam formed in his eyes. He turned to the cage door and lifted his left paw and extended it between the bars. Reaching around, he touched the door handle, and then the old lock's keyhole below it with the soft pads of his foot. He moved his paw into position, then forcefully protracted his claws. They bounced off the metal with a "clank" that echoed in the lower chamber. He moved his paw further away from the lock and tried again. "Clank," reverberated in his berth. Lefu rumbled in frustration. He made several more attempts until he heard a muffled 'ting' and he realized his claw was in the keyhole. A look of satisfaction drew across his face. He twisted and turned his claw, rotating it in the lock. He worked his paw with varied motions, but to no avail; the lock would not open.

    Tired of holding up his paw and frustrated with his efforts, he retracted his claw to remove it from the lock, but to his surprise, it only pulled his paw in closer. He twisted and jerked, pushed and pulled, but he couldn't extricate himself; his claw held fast in the lock. His anger grew with each attempt to free himself, and after several more twists and pulls, with a roar, he yanked his paw with such force that he yelped in pain when it released.

    Relieved, he pulled his aching paw back through the bars to inspect it. Although sore, it appeared okay. Exasperated, he dropped his head against the door, when another mouse squeaked. He raised his head, but it was nowhere to be seen. He then knew that it wasn't a mouse, but the squeak of the gate hinge—the door was ajar, and he was free.

Lefu stepped out of the cage and through an open door, revealing a steep staircase he'd heard Jabari climb, but never saw. At the top of the steps was another door. He stepped onto the metal staircase. It was much steeper and more awkward than what he'd climbed in the circus shows. He pressed his body flat against the stairs, while splaying his hind legs outward against the step edges. He pushed his front legs through the steps, resting on his elbows. With each step, he pulled his front paw back and over the next step, twisting his body to keep his weight in front, so he wouldn't fall.

It wasn't becoming of a lion, and it wasn't becoming of his anger. He felt the awkward and vulnerable cub inside, but it competed with the fear of being caught in such a humiliating position. Fear won as he focused on his mission, and within a few minutes he was at the top, feeling powerful once again. He was one level closer to vengeance, with any misgivings left below.

FORTY-FOUR

Lefu had lost reference to the rhythm of day and night in the ship's belly. When he pushed open the door, he was surprised to see that it was night. A thin moon hung in the sky, and the stars watched him silently as a breeze blew his mane.

The ship's engines were quieter on deck, and the sound and smell of the water now dominated his senses. He looked around warily; a dim light from a room near the front of the ship drew his attention. He prowled toward it, hoping to find the captain, but he could see through the open door the room was empty. The audience of his imagination was absent, and he'd not expected the eerie stillness. Where is everyone? He peered into the doorway of the wheelhouse, then took several cautious steps into the room, where he saw the ships wheel, tied into position with a rope.

When he concluded that whoever left would soon be back, a strange man appeared at the door. Lefu made a quick motion toward him with a deafening roar. The man's eyes grew wide in shock as fear set his body in motion. Lefu was behind the ships wheel and as he rounded the corner toward the man, his claws scratched as he slipped on the metal floor. The man dropped the cup he was holding, leaped backwards, grabbed the door and threw it shut. Lefu slammed into the door and jumped up against its window and gave another loud roar as his claws screeched on the glass. The frightened man jumped back from the lion's head, unsure of the windows strength. His face went pale and his legs trembled as he realized what he escaped, then Lefu placed his paw on the door lever. The man grabbed it and held the door shut. He caught his breath after a moment, collected himself, and shouted frantically for the captain.

Upon hearing the commotion, Jabari, who sat on the roof with O, rushed down and found Lefu in the bridge. "What are you doing there! And how did you get out!" he shouted through the glass while standing next to the man at the door.

Lefu roared and stalked around the edges of the compact room.

Intending to enter, Jabari took the handle of the helm door from the shocked man, when the captain appeared on deck. Lefu's eyes locked on the captain and he pulled his jowls back and his body tensed. His intentions were obvious to Jabari; Lefu had the same look as the day he attacked Vicente. Jabari returned the handle to the closed position and waited for the captain who walked toward him with an angry scowl. "What's going on!—No animals are allowed out!"

Jabari lifted his hands with his palms toward the captain. "I didn't let him out, and I don't know how he got out."

The captain eyed Jabari, then caught the sight of O appearing over the upper roof edge. Jabari shrank and fell silent.

The captain glowered at Jabari before turning his attention to his first mate. "Why is he there, and you here? I'm not paying a lion to steer my ship!"

The first mate stammered. "No... no sir... I... I went to the bathroom, sir just... just for a minute, and when I came back, he... he was here." He pointed to Lefu, drawing the captain's attention off himself.

The captain turned to Jabari. "Get him back in his cage!"

"Sir... it's not that simple ... I think he means harm."

The captain turned and walked away. "I'll be back."

Jabari and the first mate looked at each other, wondering what the captain intended next.

Jabari sat down and leaned his back against the bridge door. His gaze traveled up to O, and he smiled at his friend when footsteps drew his attention. It was the captain approaching with a rifle in his hand. Jabari's smile vanished, and his eyes grew wide. He sprang to his feet and took a protective stance in front of the door. The captain glowered at Jabari "I need him out, now!"

Jabari put his hands up in front of the captain to persuade him. "First let me try to get him back to his cage."

The captain patted the gunstock. "This isn't the first time that I've had to deal with animals like this—but don't worry, it's a tranquilizer."

Jabari's shoulders dropped as he exhaled, but he continued to protest, eye to eye with the captain. "I still don't want you to shoot him… besides, do you remember how hard it was to get him down the stairs last time?"

The captain hesitated, then nodded. "You have one chance." He raised the pointer finger of his free hand. "If he doesn't follow you, I will shoot him."

Jabari nodded. "Agreed." He turned his attention back to the door behind him and yelled through the glass. "Lefu, I can see that you're angry, but it's over. There's nowhere to go."

The captain positioned himself in a doorway opposite them and lifted the rifle to take aim.

Lefu paced and gave an angry growl. Jabari put his hand against the glass, pleading. "I'm trying to help you Lefu. Do you want to be shot by the captain?" Jabari looked back, drawing Lefu's attention to the gun. He didn't think it helpful to inform him there wasn't a bullet in the barrel.

FORTY-FIVE

Lefu was enraged. All his efforts only resulted in being trapped once again. As Jabari spoke, Lefu circled the room, passing the ships wheel. As he paced, he lashed out in rage and struck the rope with his claws, catching it firmly and breaking it free. The wheel whirled and the boat careened out of control, throwing Lefu against the helm wall. The captain braced himself in the doorway, his face red with anger as Jabari and the first mate were thrown to the side of the aimless ship. Jabari slammed against the ship's rail and grabbed hold of it to steady himself as he winced in pain. The ship stabilized itself in a new—though uncontrolled—direction.

Furious, Jabari marched to the helm room when the sight of O, lying on his back on the deck, caught him by surprise. He realized that the force of the sudden turn had thrown him from the roof. Jabari rushed to him, kneeled, and looked into the eyes of his dearest friend. "Are you okay?"

O's body remained motionless; his face twisted in pain. "All journey must end."

Jabari's jaw went slack and his brow furrowed, unable to accept the gravity of O's words. O smiled with his usual warm, kind eyes, and held Jabari's hand and squeezed it. In that moment, Jabari felt his friend, and understood what he meant. "No, No! You can't go!" he protested, with tears forming in his frightened eyes.

O winced in pain. "Remember stars…" The life in his eyes ebbed, then returned. "…you made of their maker."

Jabari heard the words but could not accept them. "Please, don't go," he pleaded, but he saw O's resignation. O let out a shallow breath, then his eyes became blank and lifeless. Jabari's heart sank. The world around him disappeared. He lay with his head on O's chest, clinging to him while weeping, unable to absorb what had happened so quickly.

The captain approached Jabari with his hat in hand and knelt on one knee. 'Jabari… Jabari," but he didn't respond. "Jabari," he whispered, and he rested his huge hand tenderly on Jabari's shoulder. "We must get control of the ship. I need your help to get the lion out of the helm."

Jabari lifted his head in a daze and gazed at the captain.

The captain's eyes softened, but his voice was firm. "If we don't control the ship, you will lose them all."

Jabari's thoughts turned to Ellie and Z, and he snapped out of his shock and grief. He looked up at the captain's strong eyes and took hold of his outstretched hand. Jabari stood and turned to face Lefu in the helm. "You killed O—And you will kill all of us if you don't get out of there!"

Jabari looked at the wheel now moving back and forth as the ship rocked in rhythm with it. "You have to get out of there, now!"

Lefu continued his angry pacing, and Jabari saw that he wasn't listening. He looked at the captain, exasperated.

The captain glanced at the dark waters ahead of the ship. His anxiety rose with every chug forward. "Open the door!"

Jabari looked at Lefu, then at O, and then back to the captain. No longer sorry for Lefu, he grabbed the door handle, stood to the side and swung it open, to the sound of a deafening blast. Smoke from the captain's gun wafted past his face. Jabari turned and peered into the helm room. Lefu lay slumped on the floor in front of the door, with a large dart embedded in his chest.

The captain jumped over Lefu and lunged for the throttle to stop the boat. As he grasped the lever, the ship rose on a wave, then thudded to an abrupt stop. Jabari slammed against the captain and he against the wheel with groans. Muffled protests from Ellie and Z floated up from their compartments.

The captain straightened and collected his thoughts. "She's run aground!"

The first mate raced into the helm as the captain slammed the engine into reverse and thrust the throttle, but the ship didn't move. The waves were pushing the boat against where it had run aground, negating the engine's efforts.

"Sand bar," the captain muttered under his breath. "What time is it?" he yelled, at no one in particular.

"Three a.m.," came the quick response from the first mate.

The captain studied his charts. "…Low tide and getting lower." The look of concern on the captain's face deepened as he considered their situation. "Jabari?"

"Yes sir?"

"I promised Vicente I would get you home, but your lion has made this as close as I can get your elephant."

Jabari's face went blank.

The captain pointed to a position on his chart. "We're stuck on a sand bar and the tide is getting lower. We must get the ship free. If not, we all go down."

Jabari gulped and his eyes went wide as the captain continued. "Our only hope to free the boat is to get the elephant off the ship."

Relief appeared on Jabari's face. "Ok, so we get her off and then reload her."

The captain shook his head. "I can only load when the boat is moored—I'm taking a chance offloading her while the sand holds us."

Jabari gaped at the captain. "You can't leave her out there!"

"I have no choice—" The captain pointed a finger at Ellie's compartment. "—Either she goes off the ship, or we all go off the ship!"

Jabari swallowed. "Then I'm going with her."

The captain nodded. "Okay."

A desperate look came over Jabari's face. "I can't swim."

The captain grinned. "Vicente *was* right about you."

Jabari felt anything but brave. He was terrified.

The captain pointed to a small boat hanging overhead. "You can take the life raft."

Jabari stammered, unsure to what he'd committed himself. "How... will I know... which way to go?"

The captain pointed low in the sky. "You can't see it, but we are not that far from shore. You see that bright star, low in the sky?"

Jabari's gaze followed the captain's arm. "Uh-huh."

"It will lead you to land—follow it."

Jabari looked over the dark, rolling waters and a shiver passed through him as he considered what he was going to do.

FORTY-SIX

"Prepare the hoist!" bellowed the captain into the night air. 'Aye sir!" the first mate shouted back then departed to move the boom over Ellie's hold. The captain handed Ellie's loading straps to Jabari. "Can you harness her like we did the night we loaded her?—" Jabari nodded and took the gear. "—Quickly, we can't waste any time!"

The captain and Jabari reached for the panels that covered Ellie's compartment and lifted them open and looked down at the great elephant.

Ellie looked up at Jabari with concern in her eyes. "What's going on?"

Jabari jumped onto Ellie's back, harness in hand and gave her a big hug. "We have to get off the ship early." He spoke in as optimistic a tone as he could muster, but his frantic energy betrayed his words.

"What happened? I heard a bang, then we stopped so suddenly. Are we sinking?"

Jabari draped the harness over her back. "No—Lefu took over the control room and ran the ship aground. The captain has to offload us."

"Are we all going?"

"Yes, but ... O ... O is gone."

Ellie's heart sank. "What do you mean?" she asked on a shocked inhale.

"He fell from the roof when the ship turned... he's dead because of Lefu."

Ellie's eye's burned with anger and her trunk shot up. "Lefu!"

Jabari raised a hand to calm her. "It's no use. The captain shot him with a tranquilizer. He's out cold."

"Lowering the boom!" came the abrupt notice from above, ending their conversation.

"We have to go now, Ellie." Jabari patted her back to comfort her. "I'll be with you."

Ellie saw the concern running below the surface of his words. "No, I will be with you, Jabari."

Jabari heard the solace in her words, and gave her a quick hug around her neck, before he slipped off her back and finished securing the harness. "We're going to hoist you out and put you on the sand bar where you can wait for us to join you." He then hooked the harness to the boom and shouted "Ready!" to the first mate, then rushed to Z's compartment. "Z, we have very little time—"

Z stopped Jabari mid-sentence. "I heard you talking to Ellie. I'm sorry, Jabari. I know how close you two were."

Jabari's pain rose, but he pushed it back down. "Will you come with us?"

Z held his head high. "We started together, and we'll finish together!" He caught Jabari's eye. Z's resolve comforted Jabari amidst his fear and sadness.

Jabari hugged Z's neck. "Great, we'll come and get you with the hoist in a few minutes." He affixed the harness to Z, patted him, then made his way back to the ship's deck.

"Help me load him into the boat," said the captain as Jabari appeared on deck. He'd dragged Lefu to the edge of the ship where the life raft now waited, hanging over the edge of the railing. The captain took hold of his front legs, while Jabari grasped his hind, and they slid him through the opening in the railing, and bumpily lowered him onto the floor of the small craft.

Jabari caught sight of O's body lying on the deck, then looked at the captain. "Help me get O into the boat!"

The captain furrowed his brow. "We have no time for this!"

Jabari moved toward O's body, grabbed his limp arms, and dragged him toward the lifeboat. "I'm not leaving without him!" The captain saw Jabari's determination and relented. While the first mate lifted Ellie from her compartment and into the water, the captain and Jabari carried O, resting him gently next to Lefu.

The icy water moved up Ellie's legs, sending a shiver through her body, and as she floated, the boat shifted. The deck moved under the captain and he smiled as he handed Jabari a red vest, then pointed at Ellie in the water. "I need you to release her harness."

Jabari donned the life jacket and made his way to the edge of the ship, above Ellie. He then jumped from the boat and caught hold of the hoist in mid-air. He slid down to her, reached below and undid her harness. "Ready!" shouted Jabari, and the boom and harness disappeared overhead as Jabari waited on Ellie's back. Within minutes, Z was floating through the sky above them. When he landed in the water braying, Jabari jumped onto his back and released his harness, then wrapped himself around the boom rope. "Ready!" he shouted as his adrenaline surged. It whisked him back up to the deck and for a moment, he imagined he was on the circus trapeze—but his fantasy was dashed when he looked below and saw Lefu and O in the raft.

Jabari let go of the rope and landed on the deck as the captain ordered him into the life raft and then lowered it. The sky was clear with only the dim light of the new moon shining on them. Jabari sat in the boat facing the bow, unsure of what to do. The captain looked down and motioned to Jabari. "You have to turn around!"

Jabari followed his instructions, then looked up, still unsure of what to do next.

The captain pointed to the rowlocks. "Grab the oars and put them in the rowlocks—there. Now, you row," he finished, motioning with his arms.

Jabari grasped the oars and tried the motion of rowing several times until the boat moved.

The captain shot Jabari a reassuring smile. "God be with you!" then turned and made his way to the helm.

Jabari stopped rowing and looked at Ellie and Z and pointed to the star the captain had directed him to. "We have to head toward that star. Please keep me on course and stay close." With second-hand confidence, trying his best to build their morale, he added, "Shore is not far." Then he rowed, facing the ship with his back to the star.

The captain engaged the engines and powered away. The boat became small and quiet in the distance, leaving Jabari and the animals alone in the dark, frigid water. Jabari mustered his courage and continued rowing, as Ellie and Z paddled in front of the small boat toward their beacon in the sky.

FORTY-SEVEN

With each stroke of the oars, Jabari contemplated their journey; how far they'd come, and how close they now were—yet still so far away. But his hope was darkened by sadness as he considered how much he would miss his dear friend. O had been a father to him, and now like his blood father, O too was gone. He felt alone like the small boat in the vast ocean and his grief yearned for expression, but he resisted. There's no time for this now, he thought to himself.

If not for Ellie's assurances that they were heading in the right direction, Jabari would have thought they weren't making any progress at all. A wind picked up despite the clear skies, and the water rolled with heavy swells and erratic chop, jarring the boat. Ellie had the advantage of her trunk, but Z coughed when the choppy water splashed over his head. Jabari also grew tired from the unfamiliar movement of rowing, and he saw no sign of land.

Ellie looked at her striped friend struggling in the waves. "Z, are you okay?"

"Yes... but I hope we get there soon!"

Jabari overheard them and looked back at Ellie with concern.

"Are we on track?"

Another swell lifted Ellie. "Yes, we're still heading straight for the star."

Jabari continued to pull the oars and looked at his friends from time to time but soon realized they were drifting apart.

He let go of the oars and motioned to Ellie. "I'm going to throw you a rope to help keep us together!" He turned toward the bow and pulled on the rope but discovered that Lefu's limp body was lying on it. Frustrated, he stood to pull harder, but a wave struck the side of the boat, throwing him off balance. He teetered as he tried to steady himself with the rope when a second wave followed the first and rocked the boat yet again. Fear rushed through him and he pulled the rope again to stabilize himself, when it released from under Lefu. Jabari's arms swung wildly as he tried to recapture his balance. Panicked, he let go of the line and tried to grab the edge of the small craft—but it was too late—his body tipped past the point of no return. He fell off the side of the boat and plunged into the cold water. He popped up next to the lifeboat, gasping for air—his eyes wide in panic. Never having been in water over his head, he flailed frantically—certain he would drown—until he realized the life vest was keeping him afloat. It rode high on his body with the upper portion floating at his ears, allowing the waves to splash easily against his head.

He gasped as he kicked and paddled awkwardly toward the boat, but he was unskilled, and it was drifting away from him. The immediate terror of drowning was replaced by the fear of floating alone in the water. The large waves came in succession, and the boat and his friends were disappearing between the swells. "Ellie!" he shouted. Small waves crashed around him, and large swells lifted him up and down. "Z!" he shouted.

He heard Ellie echo his name back to him, but he couldn't see from where it came, for the height of the swells. *Stay calm*, he thought to himself as he continued to paddle and kick. He called out for Ellie and Z again, and he heard Ellie trumpet his name again, but more faintly. The boat had been so close when he fell, and although he knew the wind was blowing it away, he felt like an invisible finger was pushing it. He rose atop another swell and looked for his friends for the few seconds that the crest afforded, but he couldn't see them. "Ellie, Z!" he yelled. He waited a moment for a reply, before crying out again, "Z, Ellie!"

Apart from the wind and the waves, there was only silence. Atop another swell, Jabari scanned the dimly lit sea and realized that he was alone. Gone was the raft and gone were his friends. The swell plummeted and so did Jabari's heart. Fear flooded his entire being. "Ellie…Z," he mumbled in despair. He'd never been so alone, and so afraid.

Images of his life passed through him; his childhood when he played as a boy under the watchful care of his mother and father; swinging between them while walking in their village; viewing the world from high atop his father's powerful shoulders. He'd never surveyed the depth of his life with such intensity. He knew those moments were the best of his life, and remembering them confirmed for him that this, must surely, be his end. His paddling and kicking ceased, and he cried. He slumped in his life vest like a rag doll, tears streaming from his eyes, gasping as the smaller waves splashed against his face.

The flame of his spirit was all but blown out, when he rose once again on the crest of a large swell and caught sight of the star of his destination. Upon seeing it, what was left of him—the deepest part of his essence—whispered a small, desperate prayer: "Help." The wave sank and was taking down with it the last of Jabari's will, when another long-forgotten memory returned. He saw his father sitting beside him on his bed, closed book in one hand, the other cupping his face.

Despite the icy water, the memory warmed him, and he thought for a moment that he could hear his father's voice. He first dismissed it as the wind and his imagination, but as it persisted, he became excited, hoping that the baritone sound was Z. He floated back up on a swell, and down again, but seeing nothing, he realized it wasn't the case. With his last hope dashed, he surrendered to the moment, and the familiar sound became unmistakable. It wasn't Z, and it wasn't his imagination. It was his father singing to him:

Do not be afraid; you are never alone.

We shine from above, to guide you home.
When you are troubled, look up to the light,
To find your way, through the darkest night.

Jabari's heart expanded with courage, and his strength was renewed. The dim flicker within brightened, as though a wind now blew within *him*. He'd never felt this part of himself before, but he could now feel the magic of which O had spoken. Another swell lifted him, and his spirit rose with it. With his newfound vigor, he caught sight of the star once again, and paddled toward it with all his might.

FORTY-EIGHT

Morning light penetrated Jabari's eyelids. His hands were half buried in sand and water splashed his feet. He opened his eyes and tentatively moved his limbs. His back and arms ached as he sat up to assess his surroundings. The memory of the prior night came to him: the dark frigid water, the fear, the prayer, the answer, the strength. He remembered powerful waves tossing him on the shore, before crawling up the beach and collapsing from exhaustion.

Now, shifting anxiously, he scanned the shoreline for any sign of Z, Ellie, Lefu, and O. He exhaled a sigh of sadness, remembering that O would never be with him again. With no sign of his friends, his anxiety rose higher. He ran across the beach, calling for Ellie, Z, and Lefu; first to the far side of the visible stretch of beach to its end in jungle, and then back to where he began. Winded, he looked beyond the rise of land next to him and made his way over it. "Ellie, Z, Lefu!" he called, again and again, with no response.

He climbed over a second dune and saw the small lifeboat, overturned on the shoreline. Lefu's body lay on a mound of sand beyond it. *O*, he thought to himself, as he ran toward the small craft. He grabbed its edge, squatted and put his shoulder under it and rolled the small but heavy boat over, revealing O's body. "O, my friend, my friend." He moved O's limbs and rolled him over, revealing a blank, sand covered face. Grief pierced Jabari's heart and shame flooded him for falling out of the boat, causing O's present state. His agony resumed from where he'd left it on the ship. He wiped the sand from O's face and cupped his head with his hands. "I'm sorry, my friend; I'll take care of you now," he whispered, as he cleared O's orange and gray hair from his wide face.

Jabari stood, took hold of O's hands and dragged him out of the water's edge, and onto the beach. When he let go exhausted, he saw O's arms resting over his head. Jabari couldn't help but smile through the sorrow, as he remembered all the times that O had shared with him in this same carefree position. Jabari removed his life-vest, lifted O's head, and rested it upon the red jacket. He then sat for a time beside O and surveyed the beach again for any sign of Ellie and Z. He dropped his head in despair and his heart sank with sadness as he realized that not only was he alone, but he had failed them all.

He stood to make his way toward the lifeless lion for burial, when he noticed Lefu's body rise and fall with shallow breaths, as waves lapped against his hind legs. For a fleeting moment, he was glad to see Lefu alive, but as he stepped closer, what he didn't have time to process on the ship, took hold of him. Visions of O's fading eyes came to him and Jabari's anger multiplied with each step, and by the time he reached Lefu, he was enraged.

In the absence of Z and Ellie, Jabari couldn't reconcile the fate that had befallen him. *Gone are all the good ones and left is this hateful lion.* "Why are you alive!" he shouted. "You, miserable waste—you destroyed everything!" He kicked sand at Lefu, lashing out in a breathless frenzy. "You killed O! Ellie and Z are gone, and *you* are the one left!"

Lefu remained motionless, with only the rising of his torso as evidence that he was still alive.

Large veins throbbed in Jabari's neck and forehead. "You don't deserve to live!" and as the words left his mouth, his heart filled with vengeance. He reached down with both hands and heaved a heavy rock. His body trembled and tears streaked his face as he struggled to raise it overhead. He positioned it over Lefu's mane and with an anguished scream, thrust it down with all his might. Jabari fell to his knees sobbing, sobered by the wet, crushing sound.

FORTY-NINE

"You should have done it," said the familiar voice from beside him.

Jabari ignored it.

"I deserve it...Better me than those clams."

Jabari looked at the rock next to Lefu's head and silently agreed.

"I don't deserve to live." said Lefu.

Jabari cried. He cried for the loss of his beloved friend O, and for Ellie and Z. Memories of his friends and their journey floated through him, and his heart twisted in pain. His grieving was more painful than anything he'd ever felt, and it wrenched him deeply. All the pain for his friends, now blended with an old wound deep within, never expressed; not only was he grieving the loss of his friends but was also grieving the loss of his own father. Every cell in his body ached, as he sobbed from the depths of his being, for those he'd loved, and lost.

Jabari didn't think he could endure the pain that was salted by being left with the one who'd caused it. His sobbing abated as the wave of grief passed.

"You're right...you don't deserve to live."

"Why didn't you do it?" said Lefu.

"I was about to, when O whispered to me. I heard him say, 'I okay,' like he was right beside me." Jabari exhaled a breath of relief. *I never imagined so much would be at stake*, he thought to himself, recalling O's warnings. Silence ensued as tears ran down Jabari's cheeks, and with thoughts of his father, another wave of grief swelled within him. "I miss you Akala," he blurted. The words came from deep within, releasing the wave's pressure, and he burst into sobbing again.

Lefu eyed Jabari through wet, tangled mane and waited for Jabari's tears to subside ... "What did you say?"

Jabari snorted and wiped his nose with his arm. "I told my father I miss him."

"What did you say his name was?"

"...Akala."

Something profound registered with Lefu. He looked in shock at Jabari, the energy of his glare palpable. Sensing it, Jabari turned to look him in the eye for the first time since the dreadful night on the ship. When Jabari's gaze met Lefu's, he expected anything but the shocked look he received. "You look like you've seen a ghost."

Lefu's eyes burned with intensity. "I lost my father the day I was taken from my home."

Jabari pressed a hand into the sand. "Is that why you didn't want to come back here?"

"Yeah. My name wasn't always Lefu. My mother named me Cheka. It means *Laughter*—but I haven't lived up to that name in a very long time," he said regretfully. "But before I was Lefu, the men who captured me—" he locked his gaze on Jabari. "—named me after a local man who died while trying to capture my father...until I got to the circus, my name, was *Akala*."

The look of shock left Lefu and moved to Jabari, as Lefu's revelation took hold of him. Jabari shifted from his knees and sat in the sand, with the irony of their fates crystalizing in his mind.

Lefu studied Jabari to discern what effect his disclosure was having on him.

Jabari looked at his feet, then at Lefu, and then at the crushed clams. Although the odds of their entanglement incalculable, he tried to absorb it. It was beyond belief that the lion he worked so hard to save, was the son of the lion that had killed his father. Anger rose in him again, but only briefly, remembering that he was the son of the man who'd caused Lefu's father to die. Unable to reconcile the improbabilities, he laughed. He laughed at the irony of it all, as it was both absurd and miraculous. He looked at Lefu and realized what O had said was true; they were much more than the roles they'd played; they were a part of a much bigger story. Jabari's laughter quieted, and he silently thanked O for giving him pause, as he never would've known what had entwined them. He sat quietly staring at the ocean, then looked at Lefu without disdain.

It gave Lefu courage and hope. "I have been such an angry fool. I'm sorry… I'm sorry for everything, for Ellie and Z…and O."

Jabari nodded in agreement. "You have been an angry fool but if I'd lost what you had; I might have been as angry—maybe more."

Lefu looked at Jabari with admiration. "You've been a good friend, Jabari. Far better than I deserve."

"We are all the same, Lefu… I am no better than you." As he finished the words, an enormous trumpet sound came from far down the beach, and they looked toward it.

Z ran toward them with Ellie following, blaring. The zebra kicked his hind legs into the air with excitement on each surge forward.

"They're alive!" yelled Jabari. He jumped up and ran to greet them, leaving Lefu at the water's edge. Jabari's heart was overjoyed to see them. He'd lost them, and now they were back, and it comforted him more than they could know. Exhilarated, he threw his arms with joy around Z, who couldn't keep still, and then around Ellie. Her trunk wrapped around him, squeezing tightly. Jabari's smile lit up his entire face and he danced with glee. "I thought I'd lost you!"

Ellie beamed. "We thought we'd lost you too!"

Z's infectious gummy smile brought laughter to them all. "We are soooo glad to see you Jabari!"

THE END OF THE CIRCUS

Jabari reached out to both at the same time. "I am so glad to see your faces again!" His heart was light, and he was thankful. *Thankful to have these friends. Thankful to be alive. Thankful to not have killed Lefu.*

When the moment passed, he pointed to the shore. "Lefu's alive… that's him on the beach by… O and the boat."

The three walked toward O and the lion, and their mood shifted. They stood next to O in silence, absorbing their loss together.

Ellie's anger burned. She turned toward Lefu, about to tear into him, but he spoke first: "I'm sorry, everyone. I never meant to hurt O. Ellie; you were right; I'm a coward… I'm sorry." Gone was his usual anger and his voice was absent of defense. Lefu's humility caught them off guard and disarmed Ellie. The tide was rising, and the waves that were lapping his legs were now past his torso and splashing over his face. Lefu choked and coughed. Jabari raised an eyebrow and twisted his mouth. "You can't move, can you?"

"Not a muscle."

Ellie's face became serious. "I think we should leave him here."

Z's eyes widened and his ears shifted back.

Lefu responded calmly: "I'd understand if you did." Another wave splashed over his face and he coughed again but didn't ask for help.

Ellie looked at Jabari, then at Z, and back to Lefu, who had taken yet another wave over his mouth, coughing again, without protest. Convinced he was sincere, Ellie reached down with her trunk, wrapped it around his hind leg, and lifted Lefu high into the air. His limp body drooped, and she positioned him so that his face was very near to her stern eye. "Don't make me regret this!"

Lefu looked to meet her gaze through his wet mane and held it. "I promise, I won't."

Z's worried look turned to relief, and he popped his ears back up.

Ellie set Lefu down on the dry sand, away from the water next to O. Lefu lay helpless, facing O's body stretched out before him. "I'm sorry," he whispered. "I'm so sorry."

FIFTY

They spent the morning on the beach, enjoying its smells and the warm sunshine on their bodies, while they waited for Lefu to regain control of his body. After some time, though unsteady, he lifted himself, then gazed out over the vast waters before them. "I thought I died on that ship last night... When the gun went off, everything I feared, died in me... It was like I was a cub again, hearing the shot that killed my father, only this time, it was me." They had never heard him speak this way and they looked at one another in acknowledgement, absorbing the intensity of his emotion.

Lefu held his head low. "If only I died instead." His voice was filled with remorse. No one responded as they couldn't disagree with him. Given a choice, they all preferred O.

Lefu glanced at O's body in the sand. "I would like to help bury him... if you'll let me."

His compassionate tone surprised the three friends and they looked at each other and nodded in agreement.

They took turns digging in the sand at the edge of the forest, furthest from the shore. Lefu dug more than anyone, despite his body's weakness. Confident that the hole was deep enough, Jabari and Ellie lifted O and lowered him into his resting place. They stood by the grave and the only sounds were gentle waves and a soft ocean breeze. Emotion gripped Jabari and he cleared his throat. "...You were my guide, and my best friend in..." Jabari's tears erupted, then he composed himself. He recalled their many days together: the love O had shown him; the friendship they'd shared, and the wisdom and comfort he'd given him. "You taught me the meaning of life, and you encouraged me at every turn. I will honor your memory all the days of my life."

Z's ears twitched and his lips quivered. "I wish I could have had eyes to see you sooner, O. You helped me to understand myself, and for that I am forever grateful."

Ellie waited to be sure Z was done before she put words to her feelings. "You inspired me to love myself, and that is the greatest gift anyone has ever given to me. I will remember you, always…" She sniffled, then her tears flowed, causing everyone to choke back theirs. "…Your example of love was the best teacher of all."

Lefu's mane was now dry and there were no tears in his sullen eyes. "It should have been me." He turned and walked away.

Ellie, Z, and Jabari looked at one another. The compassion of the one they were honoring, overtook Ellie. She turned her enormous body toward Lefu and stretched out her trunk and pulled his face toward her, halting him. "You can't do this Lefu!" She gazed into his eyes. "You promised you wouldn't make me regret saving you." Sensing Lefu's shame, she continued forcefully, yet compassionately, "I spent my life hating myself. If you, me, all of us, have learned anything from O, it's that we need to love ourselves, as much as each other. If you care about O like you say you do, you *have* to forgive yourself." She paused and looked at Lefu with the gentleness of a child. "*I* forgive you."

Her words cracked something hard around Lefu's heart. The pain that he held there for so many years seeped out and his eyes grew moist. He felt warm all over as his heart expanded.

Jabari held his head low and took a deep breath. Moved by her words he realized he had no place to judge. "Me too."

Lefu's tears flowed, but he tried to hold them back.

"And I," offered Z.

Lefu looked at Ellie, Z, then Jabari, and finally at O in his grave and shook his head sideways. Ellie understood his struggle, and stretched her trunk toward Lefu's face, turning his head back to her. She kept her trunk under his chin and looked at him with all the love she had. Lefu tried to look away, but she twitched her trunk, causing him to look back, and held his gaze until he could no longer resist; Lefu sobbed, openly. He held nothing back as he wailed and wept. His body shook as his stomach rolled with grief for every stolen moment of his childhood. He continued like this for a few minutes until there was nothing left to grieve. Exhausted, and with his defenses broken, love finally emerged from the young cub, and he finished with a snort followed by: "Can I have… a hug?" His trio of friends were taken aback at the uncharacteristic request, but upon realizing he was sincere, they leaped forward in unison. Z pressed his head against Lefu's mane; Ellie wrapped her trunk under his chest, and Jabari hugged his neck—his face buried in mane. Large tears spilled from Ellie's eyes and landed on Lefu's nose. Lefu looked up at her with innocent eyes, and a never-before-seen smile. Watching her tears land on his face, Ellie laughed in embarrassment, which infected them all, only to return to tears of joy begun by Lefu, followed by more deep and bonding laughter.

Lefu felt the love he'd longed for and needed his entire life. His heart was open and warm, and he had a peace he didn't think he deserved, but another gentle squeeze from Ellie's trunk pushed out the last of those thoughts. Lefu smiled to himself under the huddle as he'd never felt so good. Knowing that this was the best day of his life, he wondered why it took him so long to let it all out.

They ended their embrace and Jabari scooped up a handful of sand, stepped to O's grave and sprinkled it onto his body as a last goodbye. Following his example, Z used his nose to push a small amount over the edge, then Lefu and Ellie did the same. Ellie then filled the hole by pushing the large mound of sand into the grave, packing it firmly, but respectfully with her trunk and feet. She then located and moved a large rock over the grave—the very one that Jabari had intended to kill Lefu with. Jabari caught Lefu's eye and they smiled at the irony.

They turned and walked together on the beach; Jabari between Ellie and Z, with Lefu in front, his tail swinging from side to side. Ellie had a lightness in her step as they left the beach. "I hate to say this now, but I'm excited to be going home."

Z twitched his tail rapidly. "Me too!"

Lefu turned back with a smile. "I think O would want us to be excited," to which they smiled in return, acknowledging both his words, and his newfound warmth.

Jabari placed a hand against Ellie next to him and the other on Z's back, while gazing at Lefu. He felt the love they shared, the trust they'd built, and the friendships they'd forged. Although the thought of returning to his village filled his heart with gladness, there was a sadness to it he could not dismiss, and the thought of leaving his friends overwhelmed him. "I'm glad to be going home, but I just realized something…" Jabari paused for effect and the animals stopped and turned to hear his conclusion as he eyed each of them. "…The entire time I was with you, I was home, all along."

EPILOGUE

Ellie, Z, and Lefu pushed their noses out the windows of their transport and a warm, embracing breeze brought the unforgettable scents of the savannah to greet them. They absorbed with awe the fact that they had finally arrived. The many days of land travel allowed them to realize how far they'd come, both in distance and character. Like their joy, the dry grasslands that stretched out before them appeared to have no end. Its open skies and powerful sunshine welcomed them warmly, contrasting starkly with their many years in the confines of the circus.

They'd been here before, but they weren't the same creatures. The words 'home' and 'freedom' were now sacred, treasured sounds, that resonated with profound meaning—cultivated by years of absence and longing. Yet, for all the hardships they endured, they had no resentment or anger. There was no one to blame; the circus and its suffering were a gift that only those who'd been through it, and were now on the other side, could understand. Their journey had made them what they were now, and they wouldn't trade it for anything. They had a deep awareness and appreciation for all they'd become, because of all they'd been through.

❊ ❊ ❊

Jabari arrived at his village to great celebrations for his return, and with an appreciation for the warm acceptance of home and above all, his mother. He had grieved and healed from the loss of his father and was now grateful for all that he had. He left as an insecure boy and returned as a mature young man.

Upon reflection, which he now did often, Jabari was convinced he'd learned more from his journey than from his entire life prior. He'd learned the power of love—love from O that transformed both him and his animal friends. He'd also experienced the wonder of faith: to trust and believe the best, rather than the worst, in every situation and person. And he now understood humility, as his brush with his own darkness took him to a place that he didn't think possible; he would never again judge another. Last, and most important, he found the 'magic' inside of himself, of which O had spoken; magic that was both him, and something divine. He knew that this magic had drawn him since childhood to the circus for an adventure beyond what he could have imagined. This left him with a deep, clear knowing—an unmistakable feeling—that all of it, was his magical soul's destiny.

Inspired by the life that now flowed through him, he put his lessons to song, and at his many village gatherings, shared in verse what he'd learned. His songs softened and opened the hearts of his listeners, and he became confident with the gift of his voice; discovering for himself, that words from the 'magic inside', can indeed, change the world.

Although this brought Jabari great joy and fulfillment, his most treasured time came at the new moon, when the stars were brightest in the savannah sky. Every month at dusk, he met Ellie, Z, and now Cheka on the plain outside his village, where they watched the sky wondrously come to life. Under the glow of uncountable lights, they reminisced about their tales, and laughed about their adventures together. And always, before saying their affectionate goodbyes, knowing his father and O were there, Jabari sang to them *The Song of the Stars*:

> *We are not afraid; we are never alone.*
> *You shine from above, to guide us home.*

*When we are troubled, we look up to the light,
To find our way, through the darkest night.*

THANK YOU!

10% of the proceeds from this book have been donated to support these amazing but sadly endangered animals. If you were touched by this story, please help others to find it by posting a review on Amazon.com & Goodreads.com.

AFTERWORD

The End of the Circus came about by more than my own effort; like the tale itself, this story is also magical and bears telling...

 Many months before this story came to me, my wife asked me a simple question. "If you could wave a magic wand, what would your life look like—what would you do with your life?"

I instantly answered her. "I would love to speak to, and inspire people."

"Then do that!" she replied.

I smiled and stated what was obvious to me. "I haven't climbed Mount Everest or performed some heroic feat—I have no platform". She disagreed that I couldn't do it without having such a background, but I persisted and said that if it is meant to be, then it will happen.

Months passed and life progressed as before; I continued with the dissatisfaction of my work and while attending a meeting, I introduced a new hire with the surname of Coelho to my associates. One in the group said, "Like the author, Paulo." He then extolled the virtues of a book I had not heard of: The Alchemist.

Some weeks later, at yet another meeting, the book came up in conversation once again. I began to think that the universe was nudging me to read it so I made a note for myself to do so.

Weeks passed and I found myself standing in line for a coffee at Chicago's O'Hare Airport. The shop was in a concourse with its line of customers parallel to the high traffic corridor. As I queued in line, I noticed on the floor to the right of the person in front of me, a backpack laying a few feet into the large hallway. To my amazement, 2 feet further from that, in the busy thoroughfare, lay face up, a copy of The Alchemist. No one moved to pick it up and it was laying awkwardly, four feet into the walkway. Making things more obvious, was the fact that it was huge—a large print edition, no less! There was no ambiguity; the universe was clearly speaking to me. Inspired and excited, I wasted no time downloading and reading it.

I enjoyed it immensely, but I was disappointed. Not because the book wasn't great, but because my experience didn't match the build-up. I have been changed by books in the past without such obvious direction to read them, so it felt anticlimactic. Why had the universe so clearly guided me to this book? I tried so hard to answer this question that I found myself trying to conjure more meaning than the story itself provided. *Had I overlooked something? Am I daft?* I could not figure out what I must surely have missed.

Several more months passed, and I awoke one ordinary morning, from no ordinary dream. It was the most emotionally intense dream of my life. I felt characters so deeply, that I was sobbing as I shared them with my wife. "There is a boy who has these circus animals and he is trying to get them home," I said with tears streaming down my face "There is an angry lion, a hurt elephant, an orangutan who is the voice of wisdom, and there is a horse, but it's not a horse."

"It's a Zebra," she said knowingly.

"Of course!" I replied, stupefied by my inability to see the animal, only to feel it. My heart swelled with the emotion of each character in a way I had never felt before. Without knowing more than the basics I relayed to her, I determined that I had to write their story, and began that day.

With no experience writing anything other than business letters, marketing materials, and emails, my fears quickly decided that I was out of my league. Who am I to write a book? I don't have any writing skills. Who would even read it if I could? As these doubts began to crowd my mind from the task at hand,

I was reminded once again of The Alchemist. Ironically, it wasn't the inspirational story itself that I was reminded of, but the mere existence of the book; *Anyone can write an allegory!* I realized that I do not have to climb Mount Everest or perform an act of heroism to inspire.

I quickly searched for The Alchemist in Wikipedia and confirmed what the universe was saying to me. Paulo Coelho wrote the book in 2 weeks as it was "already written in [his] soul". Finally, I understood why I had been guided to read it (the most translated book by any living author, with over 150 million copies sold). It was pure and simple encouragement; anyone can write a work of fiction.

With this reassurance, and having been given a dream like no other, I began to write again. Writing is hard work and more so when you haven't done it before. I slogged it out part time, and after 2 years, realizing that it would take much more work than my busy work and life schedule would allow, I had another dream.

In it, I approached a field full of religious iconography—statues, stone pillars, reliefs, etc. There was an old man standing amidst them trying to sell them for a value that was much higher than anyone was willing to pay. Frustrated, he began to curse the relics and kick them and in doing so, damaged them. Seeing this, I yelled at him. "You are destroying the very things that you value so highly! If you apply some effort and make something beautiful of them, people will give you what you want!" When I awoke, I knew what it meant, and I knew the message was for me.

I am the old man. The religious icons are representative of all that I have learned—the totality of my spiritual experiences, not yet brought together into a cohesive form and hence, not valuable to anyone. I knew that I needed to take my collection of wisdom and make something beautiful of it; I needed to finish the book and I was promptly given the opportunity; later that morning, without cause, I was let go from my job of 16 years. Clearly the universe was speaking to me again, allowing me to fulfill the desire of my heart and to finish this work.

I hope the story touched you as it is my sincerest desire that like the characters, you may also be awakened to your highest self and purpose.

Michael Kares
Salt Spring Island, BC

www.michaelkares.com

ABOUT THE AUTHOR

Michael Kares

Michael is a father, lover of nature, and spiritual seeker.

He lives on Salt Spring Island, British Columbia, Canada.

Printed in Great Britain
by Amazon